The first time was when I was nineteen. I'd signed up for a weekend canoe trip in the fall semester of my sophomore year of college. I'd never been in a canoe but thought it would be a good way to meet some people.

I signed up as a non-canoe person. That meant that I didn't own a canoe and would be paired up with someone who had one and didn't have a second person for their canoe.

We met at the parking lot near the dorms at 7am on Saturday. I had a sleeping bag, some clothes, rain gear and some food in a small cooler. There was a bus waiting for us and two local canoe outfitters who had trailers designed to haul many canoes. Some of the other guys and I helped to load all of the canoes and then everyone climbed into the bus.

An hour later we were thirty miles up the Wisconsin River unloading at a boat landing. Some of the people who were already paired up began loading their canoes with their gear and the rest of us who didn't have a canoe gathered at the water's edge looking for a partner.

Many of the guys who had canoes went right to some of the un-paired girls and invited them to join them. When all of the girls were taken there were still three canoes and three riders. One of the guys looked at me and smiled. He was tall, over six feet, had thick blond hair and was very handsome. He was wearing shorts and a tank top and looked like a model.

"I'm Tyler," he said. "Want to ride with me?"

"I have to warn you, I've never been in a canoe before," I said.

"Then you won't have any bad habits that I'd have to break."

"Okay," I said, "I'm Ted."

We loaded the canoe and Tyler tied everything to the bars that ran across the middle of the canoe.

"If we tip we won't lose our stuff," he said. "The struts will keep everything safe."

Obviously the bars were struts.

Tyler took off his shoes and tied the laces around the struts. Seeing that, I did the same.

"You take the front Ted. You steer from the back so I'll take that end."

I was happy to do whatever he told me. The others had taken off one by one and we soon pushed off into the river. The water was clear and the bottom looked sandy. At first every time one of us moved I thought we were going to tip over. I grabbed the side of the canoe expecting to fall into the water.

"Just relax," Tyler said. "After a few miles you'll get your sea legs."

It was a beautiful fall day and after a while I relaxed and began enjoying the ride. We paddled a little but the river had a fast current and mostly we just rode and Tyler kept us going the right direction.

"Where are you from" Tyler asked.

"I'm from over near Milwaukee."

"Ah a big city boy," he said.

"How about you?" I asked

"I'm from a little town up near the Flambeau flowage."

"The what?"

"Have you ever heard of Lac du Flambeau?"

"Nope," I said.

"It's up near Green Bay. It's a Native American name for a lake. It means Lake of Fire. In the old days the people used torches in their canoes to travel across the lake at night and it got that name because it looked like the water was on fire."

I turned around and looked at him.

"Damn that's cool," I said.

"I have a head full of useless knowledge," he said grinning.

He'd taken off his shirt and his shorts had ridden up on his thighs. I could see up the right leg and see the head of his dick. I turned away quickly.

We paddled for several hours and soon we came to a huge sandbar where all of the canoes ahead of us had pulled up. There were half a dozen fires going and people were grilling hot dogs and other things for lunch. We pulled up and Tyler untied his cooler. I felt kind of stupid when I untied my little cooler with five bologna sandwiches in it.

"What did you bring?" Tyler asked as we walked toward one of the fires.

"I just brought some sandwiches."

I felt stupid.

"Not to worry, I brought enough for both of us and a few more. I hate to go hungry on a canoe trip."

We went to a stand of willows and cut two thin branches and stripped the leaves off of them. Then Tyler sharpened them and we each slid a wiener onto his stick. We held them over the fire and grilled them. When they both were grilled Tyler opened his cooler and pulled out two hot dog buns. We each put our wiener into a bun and then he produced mustard and pickle relish.

"Damn I feel like such a moocher," I said.

"Hey, don't worry about it Teddy. I have plenty."

He pulled out two paper bowls and a plastic container of what looked like potato salad. He dished some into each bowl and handed me one with a plastic spoon.

"Did you make this?" I asked.

"The nice lady at the deli made it."

"I'll pay for half of the stuff," I said.

He just grinned and shook his head.

"Hey Teddy, stop worrying about everything. We're here to have fun and get some nature."

We ate and sat and talked. I found out that he was a junior and lived in an apartment with two other guys.

"I'm still in a dorm," I said.

"You have more freedom in off campus housing," he said. "For instance," He said grinning as he lifted the lid of his cooler and I looked inside. There were several cans of beer under the food."

"For later," he said.

Most of the others had put out their fires and were getting back on the river. We burned our paper bowls and wiener sticks and smothered the fire. We put the coolers back in the canoe.

"Let's take a quick dip," he said.

It had gotten pretty warm and I thought that sounded like a good idea. I took my shirt off.

He looked at me. "You've got a nice body Teddy," he said.

"Oh thanks," I stammered.

"I'm going to swim naked," he said. "I hate to canoe in a wet pair of shorts."

He dropped his shorts and there he stood. His pubes were blond like his hair and they were full. His dick was long and hung down over his balls. He was circumcised and he pulled on it and seemed to stretch it out.

He stood there waiting for me. What the hell? I dropped my shorts and turned toward him. He smiled as he looked down at my cock.

"That's a dandy," he said.

I know my face turned bright red. I'm not huge but I have a pretty decent dick. I had started watching my buddies in PE class and at the pool from when I got my pubes and I knew I had an average cock or a little better. I'd trimmed my pubes once but thought that was stupid so I had a full bush too. I was also circumcised.

We both waded into the water and splashed and farted around for a while and then waded out.

Tyler began pulling the canoe off the sandbar.

"Aren't we going to put our clothes on?"

"We're the last ones," he said. "Let's canoe naked."

He gave me a crooked grin and I shrugged. I didn't mind spending the afternoon with this damn good looking guy... naked.

I'd never had sex. Well with another person present. I'd always felt awkward with girls and was terrified of the idea of doing something with another boy. It wasn't that the idea was so bad but the idea of someone finding out was horrible. So I was a nineteen year old virgin.

A couple of hours later I had to pee.

"What do I do about peeing?"

"Is it long enough to hang it over the side?"

I laughed. "Not quite."

He turned the canoe toward a sandbar. I jumped out and pulled it up. I turned my back to him and began peeing. "You've got a fine ass Teddy."

"What?"

"I said you've got a fine ass on you."

"Well thanks I guess," I said.

I pushed the canoe back off the sandbar and noticed that Tyler's dick looked a bit bigger than usual. He saw me looking at it and grinned.

We slipped our shorts on when we saw the group on the evening sandbar. We pulled up and Tyler got the tent out of the canoe. We looked around at all of the other tents and he walked off a little way from the group.

"We don't want to be in the middle of that. There will be some dope who is farting around all night keeping everyone awake and there will be fucking and sometimes that gets pretty noisy.'

We set the tent up. Then we put our sleeping bags and other clothes in the tent and joined the others at the fires to make our dinner. It turned out that Tyler had brats, buns, a can of beans and sauerkraut for the brats. We fired two each and then he opened the can of beans and put some into two more paper bowls. We sat in the sand with the group and ate. Some of the others had beer and wine and Tyler got us each a beer.

Night came and one of the guys had a guitar and began playing. Soon many sang along and it was really a very cool thing. Tyler sang and he had a beautiful voice.

"Wow, you sing well," I said.

"Thanks, this is cool huh?"

"I had no idea how nice this would be. I've been missing out on things like this."

We had three beers each and eventually the group began breaking up and everyone headed to their tents.

We walked to the edge of the river and peed and then we wiped the sand off our feet and crawled into our tent.

We both took off our shirts and zipped our sleeping bags open.

"I usually sleep nude, if you don't mind," Tyler said.

"Um, I don't mind I guess."

"Why don't you join me?"

"Well I guess I could," I said.

We both pulled our shorts off. It was still warm in the tent so we both lay on top of our sleeping bag. Tyler turned toward me and put his arm up under his head.

"Are you sure being naked doesn't bother you Teddy?"

"I guess not. I've never been naked with another guy except in PE class showers or at the pool changing room."

"Do you have a girlfriend?"

I shook my head.

"Any reason?"

"I'm awkward around girls. I never really found one that was just what I was looking for."

"So you said you've never been naked with a guy so I guess you've never been with a guy either."

"You mean for sex?"

He nodded.

"No I haven't," I said.

"Have you thought about it?"

I looked at him lying there. His face was beautiful. His body was perfect and his dick hung over his thigh.

"I've wondered," I said.

"I've been with guys," he said.

I swallowed. "Really?"

He nodded. "I'd like to be with you Teddy."

Holy shit! My heart was beating like a snare drum.

"I don't know Tyler. I've thought about it but what if someone found out?"

"Who would find out? I'm not going to tell anyone. We're here in a tent in the middle of the river and we're away from the others. Unless you scream out in pleasure no one will know."

"I have no experience."

"It's not rocket science Teddy. If you want to try, lay back and I'll show you."

I looked down and his dick was hard. It was standing out from his pubes and looked to be six or seven inches.

He saw me looking and turned on his back so his cock stood up in the air.

"Touch it if you want."

Damn, all the times I'd thought about something like this and now here I was.

"Go ahead," he said and he moved closer.

His dick was twitching like it had a heart beat of its own. I reached over and touched it. It was warm and smooth. I wrapped my hand around it. Oh man it felt amazing.

"Stroke it," Tyler said quietly.

I ran my hand up and down his hard cock. I felt my own growing. I saw Tyler look down at it.

"It seems that your cock is getting hard," he said grinning.

"This is so damn sexy," I said.

He looked at me. "May I touch it?"

I nodded.

He reached over and wrapped his hand around my cock. He gripped it and stroked it. I felt like I was going to faint.

"Do you like that?" he asked.

"It feels amazing," I said.

"I can do something else that will feel even better," he said.

I knew what he meant. I looked into his beautiful eyes and nodded.

He moved around and the next thing I felt was his warm mouth as it slid down over my cock. I thought he'd suck the head but he kept going down until his lips were touching my pubes. I felt my cock as his throat gripped it. I inhaled deeply and felt my cock throb. Oh no!

Tyler jumped when I came. I'm sure he didn't expect it. He didn't stop what he was doing. I felt my cock throbbing and knew I was filling his mouth with cum. He slid back so just the head was in his mouth and sucked on it hard. I tensed up and got a cramp in my right ass cheek. He milked the shaft and got more cum from my cock and then came up for air.

I rolled onto my belly and groaned.

"What's wrong?" he asked in alarm.

"I got a cramp in my ass cheek."

He laughed and reached over. He felt my ass and found the cramped cheek. He began massaging it and the cramp went away. I rolled back on my back and he lay down next to me.

"Damn you nearly drowned me," he said smiling.

"I didn't mean for that to happen. I'm really sorry."

"Hey, I wanted to suck you off. I just didn't expect it to happen so fast. And that cramp, I've never given a guy a cramp before."

"I guess I'm kind of special."

He put his arms around me and hugged me. I felt his hard cock pushing against mine.

"But did you like it?" he asked.

"It was fantastic. I never thought a guy's mouth would be so much better than my hand."

"Teddy there are many things that two guys can do to each other that give tons of pleasure."

"Do you want me to do it to you?"

"I don't expect it. For one thing you just came, you're out of the mood. I'm okay I can just jack off."

"That's not fair. I'll jack you off if that's okay."

He smiled and lay on his back. I moved down by his cock and looked at it. I wrapped my hand around it and began stroking it. Soon there was pre-cum on the slit.

"You're leaking," I said.

"That means you really turn me on," he said.

I looked at his cock and it looked so beautiful. I'd never seen a hard cock up close. I leaned down and smelled it. It smelled like the rest of him. I touched my nose to the side of it. Then I put my lips on the side. Oh fuck, I licked some of the pre-cum off the slit.

"Only if you want to Teddy."

I put the head of his cock in my mouth. It was smooth and soft but hard too. I licked around the rim of his head. Then I moved down and took a little more. Soon I had a third of it in my mouth.

"You're doing great," he said.

"How do you get it so far in?"

"That's an advanced technique. I'll have to show you and explain as we go."

"You just want to suck mine again."

"It's hard."

I looked down. I was hard as hell again. I got up and lay with his cock in my face and my cock in his. I felt his mouth engulf mine and I put his back in my mouth. We sucked each other for a minute.

"Okay, what you have to do is open your throat and let it slide down."

I watched as he put half of my cock in his mouth and then he tipped his head from side to side and it slid down into his throat. I felt his muscles grip it. Then he slid back off it.

"See what I did?"

I nodded. I took his cock in my mouth and when it was as far as I could get it, I opened my mouth really wide and pushed my head down on his cock. I felt it sliding into my throat and suddenly I gagged. My eyes filled with tears and I nearly threw up. I pulled off his cock.

"Sorry," I said.

"It's a learned talent. Just go slowly. I'll get off without you swallowing it like that."

We went back sucking each other. I loved the feeling and the taste of his cock in my mouth. I played with his balls and even ran my hand between his legs and squeezed his ass cheeks. He took it slowly on my cock and got me right on the edge.

I felt his cock growing even harder.

"I'm close Teddy. You don't have to let me cum in your mouth."

"I'm close too. I want to taste it."

We both got off within half a minute of each other. I came first and while I was enjoying my second orgasm his cock throbbed and I tasted his cum. He squirted several times and then dribbled. I swallowed it all.

When we'd both cum we lay there resting for a minute and then he turned my way and he wrapped his arms around me. We were lying in the dark face to face. There was enough light to see his beautiful face.

"So how do you feel about sex with guys now?"

"I think you changed my life," I said.

"What would you say about a kiss?"

I didn't reply. I put my lips on his and soon we were sucking each other's tongue.

It seemed like I'd just fallen asleep when I heard people talking outside the tent. I rolled over and saw that Tyler was awake.

"I think it's time to get going," he said.

"Short night," I said.

He grinned.

We dressed and then crawled out of the tent. The group was gathered around a cooking fire and some of the others were making breakfast. The tents were still damp from the dew so everyone ate and then cleaned up, washing, brushing teeth and such. By the time everyone was done, the tents were dry. Everyone took their tent down and soon we were all back on the water.

We paddled along quietly and I thought about the previous night. I felt kind of guilty about it. I'd thought about it many times and while Tyler and I were messing around it seemed great. But now, I was having second thoughts.

"You're pretty quiet," Tyler said.

"Just thinking," I said.

We stopped for lunch and then most of us went swimming. We put up a volley ball net on the sandbar and played for a long time. When we finished I was pooped. We paddled a few more miles and then we pulled up on a sandbar to camp for the night. Tyler said the take-out landing was only a couple of miles farther down the river so we'd make it easily in a short time in the morning.

We spent a nice evening sitting with the group singing songs and drinking some beers. A few of the others smoked some pot. Neither Tyler of I had any.

It was getting chilly so we all went to our tents. I was nervous and kind of excited about what would happen in the tent. We crawled in and wiped the sand from our feet and then Tyler got naked. He was hard. He grinned at me and looked down at his cock.

"Sorry, it's got a mind of its own."

His cock looked beautiful. I thought of the night before when I had it in my mouth.

"Well are you going to undress?" he asked.

I pulled my shirt off and then my shorts. I was partially hard. He looked at my cock and grinned. Then he reached over and took hold of it and stroked it.

"You've got a pretty dick," he said.

I swallowed hard. "You too," I said quietly.

He lay down on his side and motioned for me to lie the opposite way. I lay down so my face was at his crotch. I felt his breath on mine. Then I felt his mouth on it and he took it into his throat. I put his cock in my mouth and soon we were sucking each other greedily. I felt his hand squeezing my ass cheeks.

"Damn you've got a fine as Teddy."

"Um thank you," I said.

I felt a finger rubbing up and down the crack of my ass. Then I felt it rub my butt hole. He moved down and sucked my balls and then he pushed me on my back and lifted my legs. He moved under my balls and licked my ass crack. Suddenly I felt his tongue on my hole.

"Oh man Tyler," I whispered.

"Should I stop?"

"I'm not sure about doing that."

"Just lie there and let me make you feel nice," he said, "I won't push to fuck you, I just want to taste that pretty hole of yours."

He licked my hole and soon I felt his finger push into it. It felt amazing. He pushed his finger in and then he took my cock back in his mouth. He began to take it down his throat and suddenly I knew I was going to cum."

"I'm gonna blow Tyler."

He took me deeply again and then he shoved his finger in my ass as deep as it would go. When I came it felt like my balls were going to explode. I felt a deep throbbing in my ass that made my cock pulse so hard it hurt. He milked me out and then he lay down facing me and kissed me.

"Holy shit," I panted.

"That's pretty intense huh?"

"Damn I almost had "the big one".

He laughed. "That's your prostate," he said.

"I've heard of that."

"It's what makes guys like to get fucked."

"You've done that?"

He nodded.

"A lot?"

"Enough," he said.

"Doesn't it hurt?"

"If you loosen the guy up first with some fingers it's not so bad."

"Jeez Tyler is that why you stuck your finger in me?"

"I was just trying to make you feel good Teddy."

I lay there for a minute thinking.

"Do you want to do it to me?"

"Of course I'd love to Teddy but I don't expect it. Yesterday you were a virgin. I'm fine to just jack off."

I reached down and held his cock. It was leaking.

"Do you have protection?"

"Does a canoe with one paddle go around in circles?"

"I'll try it."

"Teddy you don't have to."

"Will you stop if it hurts too much?"

"I promise."

He rummaged in his duffle bag and came out with a condom. He rolled it down his cock and then ripped open a little tube of lube and lubed it up. He had me get on my knees and elbows and lubed my asshole too.

"I'm going to lie on my back. You straddle me and guide my cock into your ass. That way you can control it."

That sounded like a good plan to me. My cock was fully hard again. I straddled him and moved so my asshole was right over his cock. I took hold of it and squatted a bit. I felt the head touch my ass crack and moved forward a bit until it was pushing at my hole.

"Just sit?"

"Take it slowly."

His cock felt like a damn log pushing against my tight hole. I pushed down and the pressure increased. There was some pain but not so much. I pushed a little more and the pressure increased and then suddenly my ass ring opened and the head of his cock popped into my ass. Wow, that hurt!

"Holy shit," I gasped.

"If it hurts too much get off," he said.

I gritted my teeth and closed my eyes. The initial pain wasn't so bad now. I felt his fingers rubbing my nipples. That felt really nice and took my mind off my ass. I looked down at him. Damn he was a beautiful guy. I was amazed that his cock was in my ass.

I pushed a little more and it slid in deeper. It didn't hurt any worse but my ass felt full. I pushed farther and my balls were resting on his pubes. He reached over and gripped my cock. It began tingling like I was going to cum.

"Oh boy you better stop that or I'll cum," I said.

He grinned. Then he began rubbing and pinching my nipples. I began riding his cock up and down and could feel it rubbing over that pleasure spot. Each time I went over it was like a mini-orgasm.

After several minutes Tyler began to pant. "I'm going to cum," he said quietly.

I pushed down hard and his cock went deep into my ass. I felt it twitch and knew he was filling the condom. At the same time he stroked my rock hard cock and it only took about three strokes and I squirted up onto his chest. I shuddered and lay forward on top of him. He wrapped his arms around me and we kissed.

"Hot damn," I whispered.

"You like?"

"I like... I like a lot."

We lay there until his cock softened and slid out of my ass. He took the condom off and got a towel and wiped us off. We lay down body to body.

He grinned as he pecked me on the nose. "So how do you like canoe trips now?"

"If I'd have known I'd meet a gorgeous guy like you and get fucked, I'd have been going on these trips years ago."

The rest of that semester was amazing. Tyler and I got together all the time and had sex. The next time we got together I had my first experience fucking. Damn it was amazing.

We'd showered together in his place. His roommates were off to a concert so we had the place to ourselves. After we dried off we sat around naked and drank a couple of beers and soon we were fooling around playing with each other's cocks. Tyler slid his hand between my legs and rubbed my butt hole.

I did the same to him. It was really sexy to feel his little pucker.

"I want to see it," I said.

He lay back on the couch and pulled his legs up to his chest. There it was. He had a few fine blond hairs around it. I rubbed it and then I leaned down and stuck my tongue out. I touched it.

He looked up and grinned. "How's it taste?"

"Like skin."

He laughed as I leaned back down and began licking across it. Soon I was sucking his cock and had my finger in his ass.

"Let's go in the bedroom and fuck," he said.

I was so horny I ran to the bedroom. When we got there he opened his dresser and got a condom. He ripped it open and then took hold of my cock.

"What are you doing?"

"You're going to fuck me Teddy."

"I've never, you know."

"Teddy you're a college boy. This isn't rocket science. You put your wiener in my hole and let it spit."

"Well," I grinned, "I think I can master that."

It turned out that it was a little more complicated. He lay on his back with his legs up to his chest. I put my dick up to his hole and pushed. He was looser than I had been and my cock slipped right in. As soon as it was in, his butt hole clenched around the head of my cock. I instantly got the feeling and my cock began throbbing. I came.

"Oh fuck!" I groaned.

"Instantaneous ejaculation?" he said looking up and grinning.

"Damn I blew up."

I pulled the head of my dick out of his hole. The condom was a quarter full of cum.

"Let's switch places and I'll fuck you. And when we're done, you'll be ready again and you can give it another try."

This time I lay on my back like Tyler had and I liked it a lot. When we were finished my cock was hard as a hammer. I put another condom on and this time I did a lot better. Once I was inside him he wrapped his legs around me and pinched my nipples while I fucked his ass. When I came he gripped my cock with his ass ring and I nearly passed out.

Afterward we were lying naked cuddling. "There's a lot more to it than I thought," I said.

"There are little tricks. I'll be happy to teach them to you."

The end of the school year was approaching and Tyler and I hadn't talked about the future. I was head over heels in love with him and I hoped he felt the same. After classes one day I was driving over to his apartment looking forward to some hot sex. I pictured him naked in my mind and rubbed my cock. Suddenly I heard a horn blaring and glanced to my left. I was in an intersection and a city bus was bearing down on me. I lifted my foot off the gas to brake and then things went black.

"Ted... Ted."

I heard my name and it seemed like it was coming from far away.

"Ted can you hear me?"

I opened my eyes. There was a nurse looking down at me. I tried to speak but there was something in my mouth and throat.

"You have a breathing tube in your lung," she said.

I moved a bit and I thought the world was going to end. My left leg and hip hurt terribly and when I took a breath, the left side of my chest shot pain through my whole body.

"Try not to move. Your hip has been bruised very badly and you have three broken ribs. The doctor doesn't think you have any internal injuries but we'll take more tests when you feel a little better."

My mouth felt like it was full of sand. I pointed to it and she nodded.

"I can't give you water but I can let you have a few ice chips."

She put some ice in my mouth and it was like heaven. She said to relax and she left to get the doctor. Soon she came back with a man who I figured was the doctor. He checked me over.

"The accident hit your hip hard but the bone isn't broken. The hip socket is okay. We've stabilized the ball joint on the end of the femur and everything should heal nicely but it will take time. The ribs will hurt like heck for a few weeks but there's really nothing we can do about that."

I pointed to the tube in my throat.

"We'll turn down the oxygen and see if you tolerate it," he said.

The nurse did something and they both watched me like they thought I was going to stop breathing. They conferred and then the doctor said, "I'm going to take the breathing tube out."

He told me to take a deep breath and then he pulled that tube out of my throat. I gagged and thought I was going to puke all over the bed. My eyes watered and sweat broke out on my forehead but I managed not to throw up.

"That's better," I croaked.

A few hours later after I'd had some broth and a good drink of water Tyler came in. "Holy crap Teddy," he said.

I smiled. "What the hell happened?" I asked.

"They said you got hit by a damn bus."

"I was day dreaming," I said, "about you."

He smiled shyly. "I've never caused injury before."

I laughed and then cringed because it hurt my ribs like crazy.

"How long will you be in here?" he asked.

"They said two weeks or so," I said.

"Crap the semester is over in two weeks."

"I'm not going to finish," I said.

He looked uncomfortable. "I have to leave right after my last exam," he said. "I have a job that starts right away."

I reached over and he took my hand. "I'll be okay. They're going to get someone to work physical therapy with me and set me up in a ground floor apartment. The city's insurance will take care of everything."

"I feel like shit for leaving you," he said.

"It is what it is Tyler."

He stayed with me as long as he could and then he left. I lay there thinking of what a mess I was in… and then I cried.

The next morning I had to crap. I told the nurse and she said she'd get some help and be back. Soon she and another lady came in pushing what looked like an adult potty chair. They began moving wired attached to me in different places and then the other lady lifted a tube from under the covers to free it. I realized it was a catheter and it was in my dick.

Well it was like a major operation but the two of them moved me from the bed to the potty chair. After I crapped, one of them wiped my ass and then the got me back in the bed. My hip was screaming in pain and my ribs hurt like hell. I was sweating buckets.

They cleaned me up and then I fell asleep. Later they brought me some rubber eggs and half an orange. I was starving so I ate it all. I hoped I didn't have to shit again soon.

The next day a young guy came in wearing scrubs. He looked too young to be a doctor. He was about my height and had medium length sandy brown hair and deep brown eyes. He was very cute.

"I'm Eric," he said, "I'm a practical nurse."

I had no idea what that meant.

"I'm not allowed to do medical stuff. I do the basics like bathing and such," he said.

Oh wow, he was going to give me a bath.

He shut the door and pulled the curtain around my bed. Then he went into the bathroom in my room and I heard water running. Soon he came back with a pail of water and a wash rag and soap. He pulled the covers back and sat the bucket on a little stand.

"I'll have to take off your gown," he said. He unsnapped the gown and took it off. It was the first time I'd seen how black and blue I was. My whole left side was bruised.

"Wow what happened to you?" Eric asked.

"I got hit by a bus."

"No way."

I nodded. "You should see the bus."

We had a good laugh and then he began washing me. He washed my hair with the washrag and then my face and chest. Then he did my stomach and legs and feet. Then he hesitated.

"Do you want to do down there?" he asked nodding toward my dick.

"Go ahead, knock yourself out," I said.

He washed my dick and balls and down my ass crack. Then he dried everything that he'd washed.

"Now comes the hard part," he said.

He helped me roll on my right side. I nearly cried. He was very patient and gentle. When he had me on my side he washed my back and legs and my ass. Then he got the rag rinsed and washed my ass crack. He dried me off and helped me lay back.

"I'm sorry if I hurt you," he said.

"Hey it wasn't that bad. Not half as bad as the bus hitting me," I said.

He burst out laughing. Damn he was cute when he wasn't so professional acting.

He took a tube of deodorant and I lifted each arm and he put some on my armpits. Then he got a clean gown and put it on me. Then he gave me a tooth brush and toothpaste and a little plastic tray to hold under my chin and I brushed my teeth. He produced a comb and combed my hair down.

"Can I do anything else for you?"

"No I feel a hundred percent better just being cleaned up," I said.

"Your pee bag is full. I'll replace it and then I'll let you rest," he said. He changed the pee bag and then gathered up his stuff.

"Hey Eric, thanks."

He smiled.

As much as I hurt, and with a hose in my cock, I still got a little twinge thinking about this cute kid washing my dick and balls. Hot damn.

I watched TV, dozed and there was a steady stream of doctors and nurses that checked me the rest of the day. That evening I was watching some TV show and there was a light knock on the door. I said to come in.

Eric stuck his head in. "I just got off work and thought I'd stop and chat if you're not too tired."

"Hell no, I'm not tired," I said, "All I did all day was sleep between people prodding me and asking me how I feel."

He stepped in. He was wearing jeans, sneakers and a tee shirt. He brought a chair over by my bed and sat.

We talked about different things and then we hit on fishing. I found out he was from Hayward, a town in the northern part of Wisconsin. We had a lot of fishing stories to share and what seemed like a few minutes later a nurse came in with some pills for me.

"It's getting late Eric," she said.

I looked up at the clock on the wall and realized it was nearly midnight. "Wow that time flew by," I said.

"I better get going," Eric said. "I'll see you in the morning."

He left and I took my pills.

"He's a sweetie," the nurse said.

"He seems very nice. It was good to have someone my age to talk to and we're both fishermen so we're both huge liars so it worked out well."

The nurse laughed. "Men," she said.

I was hungry and hoped my breakfast was coming soon. The door opened and Eric came walking in pushing a little cart.

"Good morning," he said. "How are you feeling today?"

"I'm still really sore but improving," I said.

"I bet you'd feel better if you got that tube out of your dick."

I must have looked surprised.

"That's one of the jobs a practical nurse can do," he said. "Unless you'd rather have an RN do it."

"I'm fine with you doing it. In fact I'd rather it was a guy handling my wiener instead of a woman."

He laughed and turned the covers down. He shut off a valve on the hose coming out of the end of my dick and then he looked at me.

"This will be a little uncomfortable," he said, "It won't hurt much but there will be some pressure."

"Go ahead I'm tough," I said, "I survived getting T-boned by a bus."

He wrapped one hand around my dick and took the plastic tube in his other hand. Then he gently pulled. At first nothing happened and then the hose slipped out a little way. I inhaled. He pulled some more and in half a minute he had the hose out and had wrapped it up and had put it into a little plastic basin.

He looked at me and wiggled his eyebrows. "Okay?" he asked.

"You're hired," I said.

We both had a good laugh. He said he'd be back after I ate my breakfast for my bath. I watched his fine ass as he left the room.

"Damn I hope I don't pop a bone," I thought.

After breakfast I waited for Eric to come back. When he came into the room he had his bath stuff with him.

"Um, I need to poop," I said.

"I figured you might so I asked the head nurse and she said it was okay to get you up and use crutches to get to the bathroom. In fact the Doc wants you to start moving that hip."

He went out and came back with a pair of crutches. He lowered the side guard on the bed and helped me move to the edge. My ass hurt but it felt good to be upright.

"I'll put my arms around you and you lean onto me and we'll get you to the floor."

I nodded. He leaned into me and wrapped his arms around my chest. I could smell him and he smelled nice, like he'd just taken a shower. He leaned back and my feet slid to the floor. He held me while I got my bearings.

"Okay?" he asked.

"Stay close," I said feeling kind of wobbly.

"Don't put much weight on that left hip," he said. He put the crutches under my armpits and held me as I took a step. I felt weak but I felt great being able to move a little bit.

It took several minutes to get me to the bathroom. He untied my gown in back and positioned me over the toilet. Then he held me as I sat down on it. He left the gown over my lap.

"Do you want me to stay?"

"I'd feel safer if you did. I'd hate to fall off and break any more stuff," I said.

He grinned and stood back. I tried not to grunt too hard but my shit was hard and I really had to push. When I finally dropped a turd I also farted loudly. Eric tried not to laugh but finally we both broke out hysterically.

"Damn that raised me off the seat," I said wiping my eyes. That set us off again.

I finished and Eric had me stand up and wiped my ass. He put my gown back on me and we hobbled to the bed. He got me up on the bed and smiled at me.

"You're a trooper."

"Thanks, sorry about that fart."

He began giggling again.

"Well we might as well get your bath," he said.

He pulled the curtain around the bed and took off my gown. He began with my hair again and worked his way down. When he got to my dick and balls he washed them gently. He lifted my dick and washed the underside and then took my balls in his hand and washed them. He reached between my legs and washed my ass crack. My dick started to swell.

"Oh shit," I thought.

Eric saw my dick growing. I saw a little grin on his face. "Let's get you on your side," he said. He got me turned and washed my back and the back of my ass and legs. When he rolled me back I was fully hard. My face felt hot.

"I'm sorry," I said.

"That's okay guys get hard all the time," he said.

"It's kind of embarrassing."

"You have nothing to be embarrassed about."

"Really... you think?"

"Well I'm not an expert but that seems to be a pretty well developed one."

"You've seen a lot of them?"

"A few."

He put a clean gown on me and covered me up. He got my toothbrush and when I was settled he gathered his stuff.

"Anything else I can do for you?"

He glanced at the tent in the covers. I didn't know if he was fooling around or not.

"I'm good," I said.

"I'll stop later," he said.

He opened the door and stepped out. Before it closed he turned and winked at me.

"Damn," I said.

There were doctors and nurses in and out all day. The doc said I was healing well and he wanted me to start walking with crutches and get some movement back. After dinner the place quieted down. I was watching TV and Eric came in wearing his civilian clothes.

"Hey," I said.

"How are you feeling?"

"Better all the time," I said.

"I read your chart. They want me to get you in your shower tomorrow."

I nodded that I knew.

"So no more bed baths," I said.

"I'll still wash your back for you," he said.

He pulled over a chair and we talked. It was really nice having him there. He was so cute and so kind that I felt close to him even though we'd only met a couple of days earlier.

"So what's in your future?" Eric asked.

I shook my head. "It's kind of uncertain. I missed all of my finals so I pretty much wasted this last semester."

"You can catch up," he said.

I shrugged. I didn't know if I wanted to go back to school. Tyler was gone. I felt pretty alone.

I closed my eyes and a tear ran down my cheek. Eric took hold of my hand.

"It can't be that bad Ted."

I wiped my tears. "Eric I thought I was in love. The person I was with is gone now."

He grimaced. "I'm sorry, she must be harsh."

"It was a he Eric."

"Oh, I see," he said.

"Does it bother you?"

He shook his head. "The guy is a fool," he said.

He squeezed my hand. "I'll see you in the morning."

I'd eaten my breakfast and was kind of excited about seeing Eric. He came in wearing a pair of shorts, flip-flops and a tank top. Damn he looked amazing!

"Going to the beach?" I asked.

"No I'm going to help you in the shower."

Hot damn!

He helped me up and I wobbled to the bathroom. Eric closed the door and I heard the lock click. He kicked off his flip-flops and turned the water on. When he had it adjusted he had me hold onto two bars on the wall and took off my gown. Then he took off his shirt and helped me under the water. I held the bars while he washed my hair and did like he'd done in the bed but now, in the shower. He washed my chest and back and then knelt down and washed each leg and foot. Then he washed my ass crack and told me to turn to the side. His eyes got big when he saw my cock was fully hard.

"Wow," he said.

"Sorry."

He grinned. Then he filled his hands with liquid soap and began washing my dick and balls. He reached under my balls and washed my ass crack and butt hole. I looked down and saw a bulge in his shorts. He rinsed me off.

"So," he said.

"I haven't cum in a week," I said.

"Oh man that's bad," he said.

I looked at him and then down at my boner. He slowly reached over to it and wrapped his hand around it. He began stroking it and it only took a minute or so and I came all over the wall of the shower. He milked me out and rinsed the cum off the wall.

"Better?" he asked.

"Oh fuck yeah."

He shut the water off and dried me with a towel. Then he put a new gown on my and slipped his tank top and flip-flops back on. He helped me to the bed.

I saw that he was still hard.

"What are you going to do about that?" I asked grinning.

He made a jacking motion with his hand. "Break room," he said. "I have to go change into my scrubs," he said. He winked at me and headed for the door.

"Hey Eric," I said.

He stopped.

"I owe you one."

They took me to physical therapy later in the day. The physical therapist was a middle aged guy who showed me several stretching exercises and put me on three different machines to strengthen my leg and hip.

I was hurting when I finished and glad to get out of there. After a nap and dinner I got my crutches and hobbled up and down the hall for a while. When I finished I was ready for some sleep.

The next morning after breakfast Eric came in to bathe me.

"How was your evening?"

"My evening was okay but I went to PT yesterday."

"Ouch, those guys are torturers."

"No shit. My hip is hurting today," I said.

"I'll put some nice warm water on it in the shower and massage it for you," he said.

I eagerly followed him into the bathroom and was pleased when he locked the door. He took my gown off and I was partially hard already. He kicked off his sandals, took off his shirt and then looked at me.

"Would you be bothered if I took my pants off? I'd rather not get them wet."

I had a hard time keeping a straight face.

He pulled his pants and underwear down. I looked at his dick and balls. He was beautiful.

"Eric you're a stud," I said.

He grinned and his face turned red. He turned the water on and helped me to the grip bars on the wall. He washed my hair and then my chest and back. Then he knelt down and washed my legs and feet. My cock was now fully hard and it nearly hit him in the face as I turned toward him.

"I should have brought eye protection," he said grinning.

He stood up and his dick was hard. His bush was trimmed but not shaved. His dick was about the size of mine, six inches and it stood up in the air from his belly. His balls hung low, the left one lower than the right one.

He soaped up my dick and balls and washed them and then did my ass. I nearly came when he washed my dick.

"Do you need a little wash?" I asked.

"Well I showered this morning but it's been a while."

I grinned and squirted some soap into my right hand. I held onto the grip bar with my left. I was still wobbly and didn't want to fall on my ass. I moved closer and gripped his beautiful dick in my hand and began washing it. Then I reached under it and washed his big balls. He closed his eyes and moaned.

I washed under his balls and down his ass crack. I ran my fingers over his pucker hole and he inhaled deeply.

He took hold of my cock and we slowly jacked each other off. He came first. When I'd come he rinsed the cum off the wall and shut the water off. He got a towel and dried me off and then got another and dried himself off.

He seemed uncomfortable.

"Is there something wrong Eric?"

"I shouldn't have done that. It's very unprofessional."

"I won't tell," I said with a smirk on my face.

He put a new gown on me and dressed himself. He handed me the crutches and helped me into bed.

"Anything else you need?" he asked.

"I'm feeling pretty nice right now."

"Okay, well I have to get to my next patient."

He left the room. I wasn't sure what had gotten into him.

My doctor came in later and said I'd be able to go home the next day. I was glad to get out of the hospital but I had a problem. The dorm was closed for the summer and I had no place to live.

I started making phone calls trying to get things together so I'd have a place to go and a way to get there. I spent the rest of the day working on it.

Eric came in after dinner.

"I thought I'd stop by and see how you are?" he said.

"I can go home tomorrow but I've got a big problem."

He looked at me questioningly.

"What's the problem?"

I explained that the dorm was closed and I had no place to stay.

"My parents can't come and get me until Friday. I don't have a car so I'm kind of stuck."

I could tell he was thinking about something and making up his mind.

"You could stay with me," he said.

"Oh I can't intrude on your life."

"It's okay. The thing is that my place is just a rented room with a little kitchenette. I've got a bathroom and the rest of the place is a living room/bedroom/kitchen."

"Do you have a sofa?"

He shook his head. "I have a little table and two chairs... and a double bed."

"Oh," I said.

"You'd have to sleep in my bed with me," he said.

I smiled. "That wouldn't be so bad."

His face turned red. "Ted, I'm not gay."

My mouth dropped open. "You're not?"

He shook his head. "Yesterday when I... well you know, was the first time I ever did anything like that."

"And today?"

"I got carried away. Shit Ted I could have lost my job if anyone found out. I shouldn't have done that."

"Eric it was more my fault than yours. I just thought you were gay and took advantage of the chance to fool around with a gorgeous guy."

"You think I'm gorgeous?"

"Eric you're damn hot."

"I've thought about doing that but never had a chance before. I've dated several girls but don't have anyone I'm seeing now," he said.

"So you like girls?"

"Yeah, I do. But I've always been curious about guys."

"You might be bisexual Eric."

"Is that really something or an excuse that some guys use so they don't have to admit they're gay?"

I shrugged. "I don't know. I'm pretty new at all of this."

"You've been with other guys?"

"I've been with one other guy. That was the guy who left after his exams."

"Oh," he said.

As much as I hated to say it, I said, "If you can give me a ride tomorrow, I'll just stay at a motel for a couple of days until my parents can pick me up."

"You don't want to stay with me?"

"Eric I think it would make you uncomfortable. I think I messed you up already and you're too nice a guy to screw up."

"Ted you didn't force me to do anything. Like I said, I've thought about it before. You seemed to like me. At least your dick did," he said grinning. "I thought if I was going to approach someone, I had a good shot with you."

"So I won't be a bother if I stay with you?"

"As long as you don't fart like that in my bed we'll get along fine," he said.

We stopped at my old dorm and got my stuff. The head resident had packed it up after I called and explained my situation. When we got to Eric's place he carried my stuff in and then came back and walked with me while I hobbled into the room. It was at the back of a big house and he explained that his landlady lived in the rest of the house and was as deaf as a post.

"She's very nice though," he said grinning.

I was pretty exhausted after moving from the hospital so I lay on the bed and rested. Eric called for a pizza and sat on one of the chairs.

"I go to work at 6am," he said. I think you'll be okay while I'm gone. You can watch TV and there's food in the refrigerator."

"I'll manage," I said.

The pizza came and we ate. Afterward we both brushed our teeth and washed up. I hobbled to the side of the bed and managed to get my clothes off. I lay on the bed in my underwear. Eric came out and undressed too. He looked at me lying there and shut the light off and lay down beside me.

It was warm in the room and we didn't need a blanket.

"Is there anything I can do to make you comfortable?" he asked.

"I'm fine. This is a comfortable bed."

"I've never shared a bed before," he said.

"Even with a girl?"

He hesitated. "I've dated girls but never had sex with one," he said.

"None of my business," I said.

He lay on his side facing me.

"I guess technically I'm a virgin," he said.

"Don't feel bad. I was a virgin too until I met Tyler."

"Tell me about it."

I told him about the canoe trip and Tyler sucking my cock. Then I told him about me sucking his and the second night when we fucked.

"Was it exciting?" he asked.

"I thought I was going to have a heart attack," I said. "When I realized he wanted to suck me I almost came in my pants."

He laughed. "I think that I'd be pretty excited too."

I glanced down and in the dim light I could see a bulge in his underwear. We looked into each other's eyes.

I reached across the bed and ran my fingers down his cheek. He closed his eyes and sighed.

"Eric I don't want to do anything that would make you uncomfortable."

"You won't," he whispered.

I slid my hand down his hard stomach and to the top of his underwear. His dick was pointing up toward his belly button and the tip was sticking out of the elastic. I ran my hand down his shaft and gripped it. He gasped.

I slid my hand down inside his underwear and held onto his hard cock. I moved my hand a little and he hooked his thumbs in the elastic and shoved his underwear down to his thighs.

His dick was wet on the tip.

I moved down in the bed and held is dick upward. The tip was inches from my lips. I stuck my tongue out and licked the pre-cum off.

"Oh fuck Ted," he said quietly.

"Is it okay?"

"Damn Ted, do it, please do it."

I took the top half of his cock into my mouth. I licked around the rim and then opened my mouth and took the whole thing down into my throat. I gripped it with my throat muscles and Eric grunted. I tasted cum. I moved up so the head was in my mouth and let him unload. His cum was thick and hot. I sucked him until he squirmed away.

"Oh fuck my cock is so sensitive I can't stand it," he panted.

I kissed the tip of it and lay next to him.

He looked at me and shook his head. "That was fantastic," he said.

He looked into my eyes and leaned forward and we kissed.

His cock lay across his hip and was still thick and long but had softened up. I reached down and played with it.

"You've got a great dick," I said.

"You think?"

"It's perfect. Of course I don't have a lot of experience to compare it to."

I saw him eyeing my cock. I was hard, and the front of my underwear were tented.

"Can I?" he asked.

"If you want to," I said.

He rubbed my tits and then my belly. He slid his hand into my underwear and gripped my cock. Then he rolled my balls in his fingers.

"Your balls are bigger than mine," he said.

I shrugged.

He moved down by my dick and I lifted my ass. He shoved my underwear down to my thighs. My cock was standing up in his face.

"I know you're probably out of the mood now," I said. "You don't have to do it to me."

He glanced down at his dick. He was fully hard again.

"I'm not out of the mood Ted."

He moved his mouth up to my cock and opened it. He took most of my cock in and closed his lips around it. Then he gagged and I thought he was going to throw up.

He pulled his mouth off it and wiped his eyes.

"Too much?"

I nodded. "Go easy. It's a learned technique."

He went back to my cock and this time he sucked on the head. Then he took a little more and soon he was sucking most of it. He took it from his mouth and stuck his face in my ball sack and sucked each of them into it.

"Flip around and we'll suck each other," I said.

He switched and soon he was sucking my cock and I was back sucking his big beautiful cock. He was very enthusiastic and soon had my cock down his throat. As sexed up as I was it wasn't going to take long.

I felt my cum rising.

"I'm about to cum Eric. You don't have to take it in your mouth."

He pushed his mouth down hard over my cock and suddenly I felt his cock throb. He began cumming in my mouth and a second later I filled his eager mouth with my cum. We lay there sucking each other dry.

Then Eric turned around and lay next to me. He wrapped his arms around me and we kissed. Then he pulled me closer and I groaned.

"My ribs," I croaked.

"Oh fuck I'm so sorry Ted. I just wanted to have as much body contact as I could after that. Holy shit that was amazing."

We kissed gently. I looked into his beautiful eyes and marveled at how lucky I was.

"So you enjoyed that?

"Hell yeah," he said, "That was amazing. I've wondered what it would be like and it was way better than I imagined."

I kissed him again. "There's a lot more we can do," I said.

"I think I'm kind of done for now," he said looking at his limp cock."

"I'm talking about tomorrow."

"Does this mean I'm not a virgin any more?"

"There are advanced techniques that I need to show you to be certified non-virgin."

"Oh boy, I can't wait."

The next morning we showered together. It didn't take long and we were both hard and soon after that we took turns sucking each other off. We stopped at the McDonald's drive-thru and got breakfast sandwiches and then we went to the hospital. Eric dropped me off at the physical therapy room and I worked out there with my PT guy. We ate lunch at noon and then I rested in the PT room until Eric was finished working.

We picked up a pizza on the way back to his place, ate and then got naked and into bed. I was still very sore so we had to be careful. We made out and Eric went down on me. He looked up at me with my cock in his mouth and grinned around it.

He lay next to me and kissed. "I can't believe how wonderful sex with you is," he said.

"I was lucky to meet you," I said.

"Me too, I don't know if I'd have ever gotten the balls to do this with someone else."

"You thought you had a sure thing with me disabled?"

He laughed. "I knew if you ran I could catch you."

I ran my hands down his back and ran a finger in his ass crack. He moaned.

"Can we do some of those advanced techniques?" he asked.

"Are you sure you're ready?"

"I've never been surer of anything," he said.

We went into the shower and washed each other. Then we went back to the bed and I had him lie on his stomach. I knelt between his legs and massaged his fine ass. Then I reached under him and stroked his hard cock and big balls. I leaned down and kissed each ass cheek and then pulled them apart. His asshole was perfect. He had a few fine hairs around it and it was pink and tight. I spit on it and rubbed it. He lifted his ass in the air and I put my face in there and licked it.

"Oh man," he whispered.

I stuck my tongue into his hole and lapped at it. Then I wet a finger and slowly slipped it in. He moaned.

"You're tight," I said.

"Is that bad?"

"I need to loosen you up or it will hurt."

"I'm tough," he said.

He turned and we kissed. He lifted his hips and I worked on his ass. I slid one finger in and then another. I put three in and he was moaning. "Oh Ted do it," he said.

Then I realized it. "Shit do you have a condom?" I asked.

"Fuck no. I thought you'd have one."

"I didn't have time to shop before that bus slammed into me and I didn't know I was going to meet a guy and end up in bed with him," I said.

"Does that mean we can't do this?"

I thought for a minute.

"Do you trust me Eric?"

"Of course," he said.

"I've only fucked with Tyler and we used condoms. I've never had bareback sex."

"Obviously I haven't either," he said. "So we can do it?"

"We'd be safe."

Eric moaned when I began pushing my dick into him. He was so tight I didn't know for sure if I could get it in. I stopped pushing and he looked over his shoulder.

"What's wrong?" he asked.

"I don't want to hurt you Eric," I said.

"Will it stop eventually?"

"Eventually it will feel amazing."

"Then do it. Unless I scream like a thirteen year old girl, don't stop."

When the head finally slipped inside him he nearly hit the thirteen year old girl plateau. I stopped and let him get used to the head of my dick in his ass.

"Holy shit it feels like a fucking log," he said.

I rubbed his back and reached under him and stroked his cock. I was dripping wet.

"Should I keep going?" I asked.

"I want it all."

A few minutes later I was all the way in. Suddenly he shuddered and I knew my cock was rubbing his prostate.

"Oh man that's the spot," he said.

"Feels nice huh?"

We fucked slowly and after a few minutes I came. I slowly pulled my cock out and he turned over onto his back. He was sweating and his cock was wet with pre-cum.

"That was amazing Ted."

"I'm glad you liked it. I sure did."

He played with my limp cock. I looked down at his. "Want to fuck me now?"

"I've got to do something with that boner."

I got an idea and I carefully moved up so I was straddling his hips. I reached behind me and took his cock in my hand. I guided it up to my asshole and he grinned up at me.

"This seems like a pretty advanced technique."

"You're a fast learner," I said.

I squatted on his cock and he closed his eyes as it filled my ass. I began riding him and he reached up and rubbed my tits. My cock began growing and I got hard again. He wrapped his hand around it and jacked me slowly. It didn't take long and I felt his cock throbbing. I knew he'd cum.

I squatted down hard on it and let him fill my ass. Then he stroked me faster and I came all over his belly. I lay forward on top of him and we made out. I felt his cock slip from my ass.

We lay there in a big sweaty, slippery embrace.

"Everything I ever imagined about sex with a guy was wrong," he said.

"Was it better or worse?" I asked

"A hundred times better," he said. "I though it would be like jacking off pretty much, but this was way better."

"We need to clean up," I said.

After we showered we lay in bed naked cuddling. We kissed and played with each other's cock and balls and then we kissed some more. Damn I was falling for this guy.

"My parents will be here tomorrow," I said.

He looked stricken. "Do you have to go?"

"Eric I can't stay here. The insurance company has arranged a personal trainer to work with me to get me back to normal. I can't keep sponging off of you."

"Sponge ahead," he said. "I'd love you to stay."

"Let me get back to normal and then we'll see. I have to come back in a few weeks and get school figured out. I'm hoping they'll let me take my finals so this last semester won't be wasted."

"Will you keep in touch?"

"Of course… I'll call you every day."

He hugged me gently. "We've only known each other a few days but I feel love for you Ted."

I felt a tear come to my eye. Damn I'd been looking for a guy like this forever and now I found him and had to leave.

"I'll be back," I said in my best Arnold Schwartznegger accent.

My parents treated me like I was going to break. It took a while to make them understand that I was okay and all I needed was some physical therapy to get back in shape.

The second day I was home our insurance agent stopped by to see me. He explained that our health insurance was the best there was and it covered a personal trainer to work with me to get me over the injuries done by the bus that hit me.

He gave me a phone number and told me to call and set up something with the guy. I wasn't sure what would happen but I decided that the sooner I began working with him, the sooner I'd be back to 100% and could go back to school… and maybe to Eric.

I left a message on his machine and a half hour later he called me.

"This is Keno Hardy," he said. "You called about a personal trainer?"

I explained the situation to him and told him everything was covered by insurance.

"I work out of my home but I can make house calls," he said. "I'm doing a group class at the municipal pool on Seventh Street this afternoon. Maybe you could stop by there and we could meet and set something up," he suggested.

That sounded good so I agreed to meet him at three o'clock.

I drove to the pool and told the guy at the entrance what I was doing. He said to go in and the class was on the left end of the pool. I walked along the concrete apron around the pool and saw several old people sitting on towels doing sit-ups. There was an Asian kid standing on the corner of the pool counting for them. He was wearing a skimpy flowered Speedo and he had an ass that would stop a car. From behind he looked amazing, with big muscles, smooth dark skin and black hair cut in a messy style. He turned toward me and I nearly fell into the pool.

He was Asian and his face was a show stopper. He had deep brown eyes, almost black, and a gorgeous face. His chest was pronounced with dark nipples on his perfect pectorals, a washboard of abs and a pronounced lump in the front of his Speedo. He smiled at me and I know my mouth dropped open. His teeth were shockingly white and perfect.

"You must be Ted," he said.

I nodded dumbly.

"We're nearly finished."

I nodded again and moved to the side and sat on a lounge chair. When the old people had finished their sit-ups, he had them get into the water and they kind of marched in place. Then he told them they had done a good job and said he'd see them next week.

They all climbed out of the pool and hobbled toward the changing room.

Keno walked over to me and sat on the chair beside me. Up close he was even more gorgeous. He looked at my side. The bruises had turned from brown and black to a purple/yellow cast. He grimaced when he looked at them.

"What the hell happened to you? Get hit by a bus?"

I laughed. "That's exactly what happened," I said.

At first I don't think he believed me but eventually he realized I wasn't fooling.

"You should have seen the bus," I said.

He laughed and shook his head. "Is your hip the only thing?"

"I've got several cracked and broken ribs. They hurt like hell when I laugh or..." I was going to say have sex but stopped.

"I don't suppose you brought a suit," he said.

I shook my head.

"I'd like to get you in the pool and do some easy stretching and it's much easier if you're floating."

"I didn't think about getting in the water," I said.

"I've got an extra suit in the car. I'll go get it. Meet you in the changing room."

He trotted toward the entrance. I watched his fine ass. Holy shit.

I went into the changing room. There were benches along the walls and a shower room. I took off my shoes and socks and tee shirt. He came in from the outside door carrying a tiny little Speedo. It was just like his.

He handed it to me. It was about the size of a small envelope. I held it up and I must have had a look on my face.

He laughed. "It'll stretch," he said.

I didn't know if he was going to watch me but he didn't make a move to leave. So I stood up and dropped my shorts and underwear. He didn't hide the fact that he took a good look at my dick. I sat on the bench and put one foot and then the other in the Speedo. Then I stood up and pulled it up and over my ass and dick. It did stretch quite a bit and everything was inside when I finished. He looked at my ass and nodded.

"Very nice... it fits like a glove."

He took my clothes to the front window and we went to the pool. He jumped in but I sat on the side and then slid into the water. He stood on the bottom in the chest deep water and put his hands on my sides. He moved them up and down and put a little pressure on my left side.

"How much does that hurt?"

"It's not bad. I just have to keep from twisting a lot."

He nodded. Then he ran his hand up and down my left leg and the side of my ass. It seemed that he spent a lot of time feeling my ass. He asked me again how much pain and I said that was better than the ribs.

"Okay I think we'll work on that leg and hip first," he said.

He had me lie on my side and held his forearm and hand under my chest. Then he lifted my lower half until my leg was up on top of the water. Then he had me do a leg lift. It hurt but it wasn't terrible. We did five of those and then he moved me to my back and had me lift the leg up and down. This time he had his hand right on my middle of my ass with his fingers in my ass crack.

"Now we'll do a reverse leg lift," he said.

He maneuvered me to my belly. His upper hand was on my chest and he slid his other hand right over my cock and balls. He lifted me and I did five leg lifts. My face was inches from his. He was so damn gorgeous and he had his hand on my junk. I began to worry about popping a boner.

"Boy that's getting pretty sore," I said hoping to end things without it turning into massive erection.

He let me down in the water. He showed me what he wanted me to do with my chest. He held his left arm up in the air and than leaned to his right. That extended his side. I looked at his armpit. It had a thick patch of black hair and looked really sexy. He had me do the same and then we did the other side.

"How is the pain now?" he asked.

"I'm about ready to rest."

We got out and sat on a couple of lounge chairs. "You did well. I live only a few blocks from here. I'd like to take you home and massage those damaged muscles. After this stretching they'll tighten up but with a nice warm massage they'll stay loose."

"I have nothing else to do."

Twenty minutes later we walked into his apartment. It was neat and clean and looked like what I'd expect from a personal trainer. He had sensible furniture and one of the bedrooms had been converted into a small exercise room. We went into that room and he said to take my clothes off. I got to my underwear and he said I could keep them on if I wanted. I was still afraid of getting hard to I kept them on. He went to the other bedroom and came back wearing a loose pair of thin white shorts. They were like gymnasts wear. They didn't hide much.

I tried not to be too obvious but it was easy to see his dick hanging down a little to the left. I could see his pubic hair through the thin material. His dick swung back and forth when he moved.

He had a massage table set up and I lay on it on my belly. He had me lie on my right side and put some warm oil on my ribs. He worked them gently. His hands were soft and he knew just how to put pressure on them without hurting me. When he finished there he moved to my hip.

"Move to the side so your hip is past the edge of the table."

I did what he said.

"This would work a lot better if I take your underwear off," he said. "Your ass cheek is one huge bruise."

Holy crap!

I lifted off the table and he pulled my underwear down and off my feet. He put some of the warm oil on his hands and began massaging my ass and leg. Several times his finger tips slipped into my ass crack as he worked my ass cheek. I tried to concentrate on not getting hard. Try as I might, I felt my cock growing. Shit!

He got a towel and wiped the oil off me.

"You can sit up now," he said.

He leaned over and got my underwear. He handed them to me and I put them over my cock. I saw him glance down but he didn't say anything.

"I'll be back in a minute," he said.

He left and I quickly pulled my underwear on. I tried to hide my boner but it was futile. I grabbed my clothes and hurried into them. He came back in and smiled.

"I think you did well for your first day," he said.

"I'm a little sore but I think that helped a lot," I replied.

"Same time tomorrow?" he asked.

"That's good for me," I said.

"Just come here. We'll work out on the mat. I have a whirlpool in my bathtub and we can get you in that and get some warm water on that hip."

When I got in my car my dick was so hard it hurt. I thought of Keno in his little transparent shorts. I thought of what his dick would look like bare.

"Damn I got to get home and jack off," I thought.

That evening Eric called.

"Hey, how's the physical therapy going?" he asked.

I told him about working in the pool and the massage afterwards. I didn't tell him that my trainer was an eleven out of ten.

"When do you think you'll be back here?" he asked.

"I'm not sure what I'm going to do Eric. I have to talk to the school administration about saving my last semester. I don't have a place to live and I'm just not sure what my future will be."

"You can stay here," he quickly said. "In fact I'd love to have you here again."

I thought of us naked in his bed and my dick began getting hard.

"I had a good time there," I said quietly.

"It was an awakening for me. It was wonderful," he said.

There was a pause. I pulled my shorts and underwear down and began stroking my partially hard dick.

"What are you wearing?" he asked.

I grinned. "My shorts and underwear are around my knees and my shirt if on the bed."

"So you're playing with it?"

I said I was.

"What about you?" I asked.

"I just got out of the shower. I dried off but haven't dressed yet," he said.

I kicked my shorts and underwear off my feet. "I'm naked now too," I said.

"Are you hard?" he asked.

"Absolutely, are you?"

"Hard as a hammer," he said.

"I'd like to be there," I said, "I'd take that fine dick and slide it down my throat and squeeze your big balls."

"Oh man," he said.

"Are you making pre-cum?"

"Like a faucet," he said. "Would you lick it off?"

"I'd suck it like a lollipop."

I could hear his ragged breathing. I knew he was stroking his cock.

"I'd love to have your cock in my ass," I said.

"That was amazing Ted. I never thought something like that would feel so good. I wish you were here fucking me right now."

I felt my cock tingle.

"I'm about to cum," I said.

I lay back and squirted cum up on my belly. I grunted when I came and I heard him grunt too.

"Did you cum?" I asked.

"Damn I made a hell of a mess."

"I'd lick it up if I was there."

"Oh how I wish you were here," he whispered. "Damn Ted you've got to come back soon."

"I'm working on it Eric. I have to get well and then I'll see what I can do about the future."

"I have to take a shower," he said. "I've got cum all over myself."

"I'll think of you when I wash my dick," I said.

"Bye Ted," he said.

"Bye Eric."

I went to the shower and let the water warm up. I got in and closed the door. I let the water run over my belly onto my still partially hard dick. I closed my eyes and pictured Eric. "Damn I think I'm falling in love with that kid," I said.

Keno had me do stretching exercises. He held me from behind and I leaned over on my bad side and touched the floor. He had one hand on my hip and the other on my ass, steadying me. After several of those stretches he faced me and steadied me as I did the same thing on my upper body. He held me loosely and I stretched out. He was inches away and I could feel the heat from his strong body radiate onto me. After that I did some squats and he held my shoulders and assisted me as I stood up. Then he had me lie on the massage table and he worked my hip and side. This time he told me to take my shorts off and I lay down on the table naked. His fingers slipped into my ass crack as he massaged my ass cheek. Then I lay on my side and he carefully loosened my tight ribs. I looked down and his loose little thin shorts looked full.

"Now we should get in the whirlpool tub," he said. I followed him into the room naked. He turned on the spigots and I stood there partially hard. He tested the water with his hand.

"It's okay," he said. Then he surprised me. He slipped his little shorts off. His dick was perfect, just like I'd expected it to be. He was cut and his dick was thick and about three inches. His pubic hair was black and silky and very straight and loose. His balls were smooth and hung down a couple of inches.

"I'll sit on the seat and you can lean back against me. That way I can massage your ribs," he said.

He got in the tub and held his hand up so I could use it to steady myself. I got in and sat against his belly. He pulled me back and put his arms around me. He softly rubbed my side and it felt amazing. He turned on the jets of water and the stream gently pumped the water against my side. I leaned back more and could feel his dick in my ass crack. His firm body felt amazing against my back. We sat like that for about ten minutes and then he had me lay across his lap so my hip was in front of the water jet. While the water streamed against my hip he massaged it gently. His dick was right under my left armpit. His hand strayed into my ass crack again and I closed my eyes with pleasure.

"You are enjoying it?" he asked.

"It's wonderful."

"You have a nice body," he said.

"Not like yours."

He smiled. "I work very hard on my body."

"It's beautiful," I said. Oops did I really say that?

Now he was running his fingers up and down my ass crack and hot trying to make it look like it was just a mistake.

"I can feel your penis," he said. "You are hard."

"It's impossible to be in a place like this with a beautiful guy like you and not get hard," I said.

I felt his hand slide under my belly and down to my crotch. He gripped my cock and stroked it.

"Does that bother you?" he asked.

"Oh hell no," I said.

I moved and turned on my back. My dick was standing up in the air and he was jacking me. I reached down and found his dick. It was hard.

"Perhaps we should go to the other room," he said.

We stood up. I looked at his dick. It was a little shorter than mine but it was thick. The head was like a big strawberry. We dried off and I thought we were going to the massage room but he steered me to his bedroom.

We lay on the bed and explored each other. He lay back and let me touch him all over. I sucked his nipples and then kissed his belly. I went down past his crotch and kissed each of his toes and the sole of each foot. Then I worked my way up kissing his knees and thighs and then his balls. I looked up at him. He was watching me and smiling.

I took his dick in my fingers and put the head in my mouth. I sucked the head for a minute and then took the whole thing down my throat. He gasped.

"Oh Ted, you have experience."

"This isn't my first time but I'm not real experienced," I said.

"You must be a fast learner."

I smiled and took him down my throat again. He held my head and let me suck him for several minutes.

"I want to suck you," he whispered.

I rolled off him and he knelt between my legs. He took my dick in his hand and licked the underside of it. Then he sucked each of my balls. He went back to my dick and took most of it down his throat.

After several minutes he flipped around and we sucked each other. We took our time and after many minutes I heard him grunt and tasted cum. I took his cock deep and let him fill my throat. He kept sucking me and I felt the tingle. My cock throbbed and I came in his mouth. He sucked on the head of my dick and I nearly passed out from the feeling.

Afterward we lay side by side, still naked. "I don't usually do that with a client," he said.

"But with me?"

"I had a feeling you were interested."

"Are most of your clients my age?"

He grinned. "Most are old and wrinkled and have nuts that hang half way to their knee."

"Well I'm glad you had that feeling," I said.

"Me too."

That night in my room at my parent's house I thought about Eric and felt guilty. It wasn't like we were long time boyfriends or going steady but I had feelings for him. With Keno it was pure unadulterated sex. He had a perfect body, perfect face and a hell of a nice cock. I couldn't wait until the next day for my appointment.

The next day Keno answered the door wearing his tiny shorts. He smiled and led me to the workout room. He gently massaged my hip and leg and then we did stretching exercises to loosen up my ribs.

"Your bruises are fading," he said.

I nodded. "They're not black anymore, more like a deep purple."

He laughed.

"So," he said, "time for a whirlpool."

I began getting hard immediately. He filled the tub and when it was ready I undressed fully. My cock was standing up hard and ready. He removed his little shorts and he was hard too. We got in the tub and he sat back and I sat against him. I could feel his cock between my ass cheeks.

I leaned into him and he put his arms around me and rubbed my nipples. Then he slid his hands down and gripped my cock.

"Are you a top or bottom?"

"Both," I said.

He kissed my cheek. I moved off him and sat at the other end of the tub and he leaned down and sucked my cock. Then he got to his knees and moved up to me and I sucked his perfect thick cock.

"Would you like to fuck me?" he asked quietly.

"I'd love to," I said.

He reached up to a shelf with shampoo and a package of condoms on it. He ripped one open and rolled it down my cock.

"How would you like me?" he asked.

"On your knees."

He turned and there was his prefect ass sticking up. I ran my finger down it and leaned in and stuck my tongue into his ass pucker. He had a few fine hairs surrounding it. I lapped it for a few minutes and then I put my dick head up to it. He was tight but I worked my cock into him. I began fucking him slowly.

"Your cock is perfect," he said.

"I'm glad you like it. Have you done this a lot?"

"No, I'm not a virgin but I've been very careful."

I didn't know what he meant but I was busy at the moment. I fucked him slowly until I got close and then I sped up and came hard into the condom. I took the condom off and we lay in the warm water together.

"My parents are very conservative. If they had any inkling that I was having sex with a boy they'd disown me."

"Are they here in America?"

"Yes they both were born here, as was I. They are just of the old school."

"So you've never had a boyfriend?"

He shrugged. "I had a wonderful friend when I was going to school to learn massage and exercises. We became very intimate but he wanted more and I had to say no. That was the end of our time together."

"That's too bad," I said. "I won't tell."

He grinned. He reached up and ripped another condom open. He rolled it down his cock.

"We must be careful," he said. "I don't want to hurt you."

"I've had bigger dicks," I said grinning.

"I meant I don't want to hurt your injuries," he said looking a little pissed.

I laughed. "I know what you meant, I was just messing with you."

"I know I have a small dick. Asian guys usually do have smaller ones."

"It's perfect Keno," I said.

We ended up with me on my knees. He licked my hole and then fucked me gently. When we finished we showered together. He kissed me at the door and I said I'd see him the next day.

"I have news," Eric said.

"I hope its good news."

"Well it could be. I've found a nice small apartment. It's nicer than my present one but I'd need a roommate if I got it."

"So did you post something in Craigs List?"

"No."

"Did you make posters and tack them to street poles?"

"No!"

I was trying to keep from bursting out laughing.

"You fucker!" he said.

I began laughing. "Are you asking me to live with you?"

"Well that was the idea but now I'm not so sure."

"Wow, touchy," I said.

"There's only one bedroom," he said. "We'd have to share a bed."

"I'm out," I said.

"Huh?"

"Just kidding. I'd love to sleep with you again and again. How soon do you have to decide?"

"The landlord said he'd hold it for a week."

"I have to call the school and make sure about classes and how to finish this year. I'll do that first thing in the morning and let you know tomorrow."

"How's the therapy coming?"

"I'm getting there. The guy is really great. His hands are like magic."

I didn't tell him about his mouth and ass.

"Are you horny now?" Eric asked.

I grinned. "It just so happens that I am. What are you wearing?"

Ten minutes later I got in the shower and rinsed the cum off my belly. I dried off and lay naked on my bed. I felt a little guilty for fucking around with Keno but it wasn't anything but random sex. But Eric... damn I liked that guy. I liked him a lot.

Two weeks later I went for my last massage therapy with Keno. We skipped massage and went right to the whirlpool. There was no pretense about therapy. We were there for the sex.

I lay on my back and he squatted on my cock. His boner was bouncing up and down as he rode it. I reached up and rubbed his fine nipples. He groaned.

"Jack me," he said.

I took hold of his cock and slowly stroked it. Pre-cum oozed out onto my hand. He rode me and I jacked him and we timed it almost perfectly. I came just a half a minute before he did. He lay on top of me and we kissed.

"A perfect way to end this," he said.

"I'll miss you," I said.

He nodded. "I will miss you too."

"If I ever get hit by a bus again, I'll request you as my personal trainer."

He laughed. "You don't have to get hit by a bus, just call if you ever need a massage."

"I'll keep that in mind," I said.

My heart was heavy as I drove home. I'd become fond of him. I hoped he found someone who he could fall in love with.

I drove back to school and found the apartment. Eric had given me directions and I knocked at the door. I heard someone moving inside and suddenly the door opened and there Eric stood, stark naked, sporting a hard on.

"Greetings," he said.

My clothes were strewn across the floor on the way to the bedroom. We had hot, passionate sex and afterward we lay there cuddling.

"Damn I've missed you," he said.

"I've thought about you every day," I answered.

We kissed and soon we were groping each other. Eric was already hard a second time and he fucked me again. By the time we were finished I was ready for a second one too. We ended up at four times each before we decided it was time for dinner.

I looked over the apartment as I walked out of the bedroom. "This is nice," I said.

He laughed. We kind of skipped the grand tour," he said.

"We had some serious fucking to do," I said.

We ordered pizza and carried my stuff in. After we ate we showered and that led to another double fuck.

"We're going to have to get tested," Eric said. "We can't keep using condoms at this pace or we'll go broke."

I took my finals from the previous semester the next three days. Then I registered for the upcoming semester. Eric went to work and when he came home we had sex. We did it every way conceivable. We did it on the kitchen table and in the shower and once, on the little deck off the kitchen. It was dark outside though.

We lay in bed cooling off after our first bareback sex. We'd been tested and both were clean. Eric looked at me and smiled.

"Happy?" I said.

"Ecstatic."

"Did you like the bare sex better?"

He looked like he was thinking hard. "I know there was a difference. I'm just not sure if it was better or not."

"I wondered about that too. Maybe we should do it again and go slower, for comparison purposes."

"That's a good idea."

We burst out laughing. "Top or bottom" he asked.

My Eighteenth Summer

The summer I turned 18 was one that I'll never forget. I was a typical teenage boy that could get a boner in a minute and I seemed to have one most of the time. My cock had grown from a little thing to pee with into a handful of thick meat that gave me hours of erotic fun. I'd become very fond of running naked in the woods around town. I'd ride my bike down to a public area woods, hide the bike in the bushes and then take off my clothes and walk around with a big boner stroking myself until I shot my sperm all over some bushes. This was almost a daily habit and it got to the point that it was almost all I could think about.

The only problem with it was that summer mosquitoes just about ate me alive in the thick woods. That kind of took the fun out of getting naked there.

After many weeks of naked hikes in the woods I started swimming out to a sandbar in the river and getting naked there. These sandbars had small willows growing on them so I had a place to walk around and lay on the sand without someone seeing me. I spent hours naked exploring in the sand, pretending I was on some deserted island. In fact I was naked so much that my ass and dick became very tan. I lost any tan-line I'd gotten from wearing a swimming suit at the local public pool.

One day I went to the public swimming pool and went swimming with some of my friends. These were guys I'd grown up with and a few of them were more than that. I'd messed with some of them jacking off. I really wanted to suck their dicks but was afraid to ask for fear of being labeled a queer. None of them knew of my naked playing on the sandbars.

There were several college kids who ran the changing house and were lifeguards at the pool. There was one lifeguard who caught my eye. He was a tall kid with long curly brown hair and a body that an eighteen year old could only dream about. He had a great looking face and deep brown eyes and was very friendly to the kids in the pool. I found out that his name was Mark. He often sat on a tall chair at the deep end of the pool watching the kids swim. If you went past him, his feet were about at eye level for a person on the ground. He had the prettiest feet I'd ever seen and I got in and out of the pool a lot right there so I could look at them.

I don't know why his feet turned me on but they did and I often got a boner looking at them. One of my friends and I were sleeping out in my tent one time and we ended up jacking off together. For some reason, while we were jacking off he rubbed my cock with the sole of his foot. Man that turned me on and I came all over it. He thought it was hilarious. I thought it was hot as hell and jacked off to the memory many times.

That day I climbed up to the high diving board and Mark looked up at me.

"Hey lets see a half twist."

"I'm not sure I can do it but I'll try," I said.

I walked to the end of the board and jumped to make it spring and then dove off trying to twist as I plummeted to the water. I got about a quarter of the way around and hit the water at kind of a bad angle. I went to the bottom, pushed off and started to the surface when I felt my cock moving like it was free in the water. I looked down and my swimming suit was missing!

I came to the top and Mark was looking at me. He grinned.

"Nice dive, but I think you lost something."

"No shit," I said. I was looking down into the water.

"Over there," he said pointing. I looked where he pointed and saw my suit down on the bottom. I swam over to it, dove down and grabbed it but couldn't get it on while treading water so I swam over next to Mark and hung onto the ladder as I pulled my suit up. I climbed out of the pool next to Mark's pretty feet and looked up at him. He grinned and wiggled his eyebrows.

"Where do you swim when you're not here?" he said quietly.

"I go to the river a lot, why?"

"I noticed your cute little butt is as tan as hell. Do you skinny dip?"

I grinned. "Yeah, I like to swim naked most of the time."

Mark nodded his head and smiled.

"Nice ass," he said.

I felt my face getting warm and my dick twitched. Maybe Mark would like to play.

A couple of hours later I decided to go home and went to the changing room. I stripped off my suit and went into the shower to rinse off the chlorine from the pool. As I was walking from the shower room Mark walked into the changing room. He stood there watching me walk toward him, his eyes glued to my cock, which was swinging in front of my crotch.

He smiled. "Nice," he said.

I didn't know what to say but my cock immediately began to bone up. I turned to hide it.

"Don't worry, I'm cool with it," Mark said. He lowered his voice, "In fact, I'd like to see it."

I finished drying off and my cock was hard and sticking straight out. I turned and faced Mark. He took a deep breath.

"Oh yeah, that's nice," he said.

I didn't know what to say so I said, "thanks."

Mark walked to the doorway and looked out. Then he walked back to me and pulled down the front of his swimming suit. His big boner popped out, hard as a rock.

"What do you think?" he asked.

I was mesmerized. "It's big," was all I could say. It had to be close to seven inches long and really thick. I reached for it.

"Not here," he said. "I'm off tomorrow, how about you and I go swimming in the river tomorrow?"

I nodded yes. "I'll meet you here about noon."

He tucked that big cock into his trunks and wrapped a towel around his waist. He grinned at me and winked and then walked back out to the pool.

That night I jacked off three times thinking about Mark's big cock. It was at least a couple of inches longer than my 5 1/2 inches and about the same thickness. He had a thick brown bush and his balls hung down real loose and looked as big as walnuts. It was a long night.

The next day I was at the pool right at noon. Mark drove up in a nice car and motioned for me to get in. I left my bike in the bike stand and we drove off toward the river. I told Mark where I usually swam naked and we drove there and parked the car. We swam across the channel to the sandbar, walked into the willows and stopped. Mark turned to me.

"Is it ok if I take off your swimming suit?"

I nodded.

He stepped up to me and hooked his thumbs into my suit and pulled it to the sand. My cock was hard and sticking out. Mark knelt in the sand and put his hand on it. I jumped a little as he jacked it until a big clear drop of pre-cum oozed out. He leaned forward and licked it off. I closed my eyes as he engulfed my cock with his mouth. He swirled his tongue around the head and then sucked it all the way to my pubes. My knees started to shake.

"Mark I'm gonna cum if you keep doing that. I don't want to cum so quickly."

Mark took my cock from his mouth and stood up.

"Get it out," he said.

I took hold of Mark's suit and pulled it down. His big cock was hooked under the elastic and sprung up like a spring pole when it came past the elastic.

I'd dreamt of sucking a cock for a long time. I think I knew from about 8th grade that I liked boys better than girls. When I jacked off the first time it was after gym class and I'd gotten to see my buddy's bare cocks and it was such a turn-on. I knew from then on that I wanted to taste a cock but was terrified to try it with one of my friends for fear it would get out that I was gay.

Now here I was with a college guy who wanted me to suck him. I knelt on the sand and looked at his cock. It was only inches from my face so I leaned forward and put my lips on the head. Mark took a breath as I put the head into my mouth.

Oh man, it was everything I'd imagined it would be. The head was smooth and hot against my tongue. I put my lips around it and licked the slit with my tongue. Then I tried to suck it all the way down. I gagged. I took it out of my mouth and tried again but it was too long and I could only get about half in my mouth.

"Go slow, you don't need to get it all the way in," Mark said.

I sucked on it and played with his big balls and soon he was moaning.

"Slow down, I don't want to cum too soon," he said. I let his cock loose and stood up.

Mark put his arm around me and we walked slowly through the willows and just groped each other. He had his hand on my ass and rubbed my butt cheeks and ran his finger up and down my butt crack. It felt amazing. It was so erotic to think this beautiful college guy was interested in plain old me.

We waded into the water a while and then lay on the damp sand at the water's edge. I looked down at Mark's beautiful feet in the edge of the water and longed to touch them.

"Mark, can I, um, I like your feet, is it ok if I touch them?"

Mark grinned. "You're into feet? Cool, sure, go for it."

He lifted his feet from the water and I sat down by them and he put them into my lap. His feet were touching my cock and balls as he wiggled his toes and grinned at me. I took his feet and massaged them and then put his big toe into my mouth. I kissed his feet and sucked his toes and Mark was getting into it. My cock was throbbing and as hard as it had ever been. I moved a little so I was facing Mark and took his feet and put one of them on each side of my cock. Then I grasped his toes together and began to move his feet up and down over my cock.

Mark grinned. "A foot jack-off," he said.

I held his feet together and Mark moved them up and down and soon I felt my cock begin to tickle.

"Do it faster Mark, I'm gonna cum."

Mark squeezed harder and soon my cock exploded and cum shot all over his feet and my hands. Mark milked my cock until it stopped dribbling.

I lifted his feet up and licked my cum off them. Then Mark took my hands and licked the remaining cum off them.

"Umm, sweet boy cum," he said.

When my hands were clean Mark lay back in the sand with his big cock standing up. He looked down at his cock and at me.

"Still in the mood?" he asked.

I nodded and knelt between Mark's legs and sucked his cock into my mouth. I bobbed up and down on that big cock and Mark played with my hair and ears. Soon he began to moan and I felt his cock throb and then tasted his cum shooting into my mouth. I sucked every drop from it and licked it clean as Mark laid back and caught his breath.

I lay down next to Mark and looked over at him.

"Thanks Mark, that was fantastic."

He smiled at me. "You don't have to thank me, I should thank you."

"I'm happy that you like me Mark," I said.

"What's not to like? You're a gorgeous boy."

"Oh I'm not gorgeous like you are Mark. I'm just plain."

"Danny, you're a great looking kid. Whoever told you that you're plain is just wrong. You've got a great body for a kid your age and a really nice face and beautiful eyes. And you've got a hell of a cock on you too."

Then he looked down at my cock.

"Shit you're hard again. Damn to be eighteen again."

I grinned. Mark leaned over and sucked my cock into his mouth and it wasn't long and I was pumping my second orgasm into his mouth. Mark cleaned up my cock and we lay there together in the sun and went to sleep, naked and very satisfied. When I woke up Mark had his arms around me and was sleeping. I leaned over and kissed his handsome face and snuggled down into his arms. I'd never kissed another guy before and I had wanted to do it for a long time. It was easier since he was sleeping. I snuggled up against him. I wasn't in any hurry to go back from this perfect place.

I drifted off to sleep and woke when Mark put my dick into his mouth. He must have been playing with it because I was hard already. He sucked me deeply and it didn't take long for me to cum.

Mark lay down next to me again and kissed me lightly.

"I'm sure glad you lost your swimming suit the other day," he said.

"Why is that?"

"Because it gave me a reason to get to talk to you and that turned into a fun day being naked."

"I'm glad too," I said. "But I owe you a cum right now don't I?"

"Fuck, I lost track," he said laughing.

"Well, just in case," I said.

I got up and knelt between Mark's legs and began licking his balls and sucking his dick. He boned up in no time and soon I was taking his cock deep into my throat. I found how to open my throat and let it slide down it without gagging and Mark gasped when I did it. He began moaning and soon he clenched up and shot cum into my throat. I milked him dry and then lay on top of him.

"There, debt paid," I said.

"Damn you're one hot kid," he said.

We got up and walked back to where our swimming suits were laying in the sand. We put them on and swam back to shore.

"See you tomorrow?" Mark asked as I got out of his car.

"Definitely," I said.

My friend Tommy was just getting on his bike at the pool when Mark and I drove up. I got out of his car and walked to my bike.

"Where were you?" Tommy asked.

"Huh? Oh I was just taking a ride with Mark," I said. I wasn't very convincing because Tommy looked at me funny.

"Taking a ride where?"

"He was just showing me his car."

"Uh huh."

I went home and after dinner I went out to the back yard and built a fire in the fire circle out back by my tent. I'd put up a tent in the back yard earlier in the summer and slept out there a lot during the nice weather. I had a metal ring on the ground and it was for having a campfire. After my day of naked fun with Mark I felt like sleeping in the tent for some reason.

I was sitting in a lawn lounge chair poking a stick into the fire when I heard a bike rattle in the alley behind the yard.

"Who's that?" I said.

"Just me."

It was Tommy. He came walking up through the dark.

"What's up?" I asked.

He shrugged.

"I saw your fire back here. I just thought you might like some company."

"Sure… have a chair," I said gesturing to another chair.

We made small talk about fishing and stuff for a while and then it got silent.

"So Danny, what were you really doing with the lifeguard?"

"Why is it so important to know what I was doing?"

"I noticed the other day you spent a lot of time talking to him at the pool. Are you guys friends?"

"I guess so."

"We're friends aren't we?"

"Sure Tommy. We've grown up together. We've fished and played ball and stuff together from grade school on. I think we're good friends, same age, same interests."

"So why are you lying to me?"

I didn't know what to say. Tommy had been like a brother to me for years. We'd fished and hunted together, and slept over at each other's houses many times.

I looked at him sitting there with the light from the fire dancing across his face and realized just how good looking he had become. When we were boys we were both kind of skinny and geek-like but now we were young men and things had changed. Tommy was a cute guy. He had dark brown hair that he kept short and preppy, dark brown eyes and had a killer body. I'd seen him naked when we were kids but hadn't since puberty set in. I began to wonder where he was going with the questions.

"Tommy we're all grown up now. I've got things in my life that you might not understand."

"Try me."

"I can't Tommy. I want us to be friends and if I tell you this I'm afraid we might not be friends any more."

"Is it sex?"

Wow, he knew.

"I'm not the same as you Tommy." I took a deep breath and continued, "I've figured out that I'm attracted to boys, not girls like you are."

He sat there for quite a while.

"Did you and Mark do stuff?"

I nodded.

"Like what?"

My face got hot.

"We went to that sandbar with all the willows on it. And we got naked and played with each other's cocks."

"No shit?"

I nodded.

"Is that all you did?"

"We sucked each other off."

"You sucked his cock?"

I nodded again.

"Holy shit."

I expected him to get up and leave and our friendship would be over.

"What was it like?"

Whoa! I didn't expect that.

"It just happened Tommy. One minute we were pulling on each other's cocks and the next we were sucking each other."

"Oh man. What did it taste like?"

He arranged his dick in his pants.

"It tastes like skin. Mark has a big cock and it's really sexy and it was the most erotic thing I've ever done," I said.

"And he sucked you too? Was it good?"

"It was ten times better than jacking off."

"I've always wondered about doing that," he said.

"Really? I thought you were chasing pussy."

He smiled widely.

"You know Jessica? I fucked her."

"No shit? When?"

"At Homecoming last year. We went to a party after the game and she let me feel her pussy. I stuck my hand down her pants and stuck my finger in it. She got out my cock and the next thing I knew we were fucking in the back seat of Joey's car."

"Damn Tommy. How was it?"

"Short. I came about a minute after I put it in."

I laughed.

"Oh well, at least you fucked her," I said.

"Yeah, but it wasn't all that great. That stuff you did with Mark makes me pretty horny."

"You got a boner?"

He nodded. He stroked it under his shorts.

"How about you?" he asked.

I took hold of my boner and showed it to him through my shorts.

"Looks big," he said.

"It's pretty big. How about yours?"

"It's 5 and ¾ inches," he said.

"You measured?"

He nodded and grinned.

"Want to see?"

My heart began beating faster. This was a big step.

"Let's go in the tent," I said.

We crawled into the tent and zipped the door shut. I turned on a little battery operated light. We were kneeling on an open sleeping bag.

Neither of us said anything. We both unzipped our shorts and let them fall to the ground. Then we both dropped our boxers.

Wow, Tommy's cock was nice. It was standing up next to his belly and the head on it was wet. His balls hung down loose and his pubic bush was thick and dark like his hair on his head.

He looked at my cock.

"Damn yours is fat," he said.

"Touch it if you want," I whispered.

Tommy hesitated and then he reached over and put his hand on my cock. I closed my eyes and enjoyed the feeling of his hand as he stroked it.

"Do me," he said.

I took hold of Tommy's cock and it felt like it was on fire. It was hard as a stone and I ran my hand up and down his shaft. Pre-cum oozed out of the head.

"Oh Danny, that feels so good," he said.

"I can do something that will feel better if you want," I said.

He looked me in the eye. He nodded.

"Stand up," I said.

I leaned forward and pulled his cock away from his belly. The tip was all wet with pre-cum. I stuck my tongue out and licked it off. Tommy gasped.

I opened my mouth and took about half of his cock into it.

"Oh God!" he whispered.

I took his cock down my throat and closed my lips around it right at his pubes. I slid up the shaft to the head and then slid back down to his pubes. Tommy groaned and suddenly my mouth was full of cum.

"Oh fuck," he gasped.

I sucked his dick head until it stopped squirting cum and then milked the shaft getting every last drop.

"Oh man Danny, I'm so sorry. I didn't mean to cum in your mouth," he said.

"It's okay Tommy. I liked it."

"You swallowed it?"

I nodded.

"What's it taste like?"

I took my cock in my hand and looked at him.

"Here, try it and see."

I stood up and he knelt on the floor of the tent. He looked apprehensive but he bent down and took my cock in his hand. He leaned forward and smelled it.

"Smells nice," he said.

Then he opened his mouth and put the head in. I could feel his tongue licking it. He seemed to like that because he went farther down on it. He was about half way when he gagged.

"Tommy, don't go too far. Just take it as far as you can without gagging."

He nodded and went back to it. Soon he was bobbing up and down on it like a pro. He took it from his mouth and sucked on my balls and then put it back in and slurped on the head.

"I'm almost there," I said. "If you don't want me to cum in your mouth just take it out and jack me off."

He kept sucking me.

"Tommy its cumming."

He held my cock in his mouth and let me cum. I could see he was swallowing. When I stopped cumming he sucked it all clean and took it from his mouth.

"Wow," he said.

"What do you think?" I asked.

"I think we should have done that years ago," he said.

"You liked it?"

"Fucking right I liked it. I was afraid it would be nasty and stinky but it's not. Cum has a strange taste but its okay. Damn Danny that was amazing."

I knelt back down in front of him. He moved forward and put his arms around me. Our semi-hard cocks were pushing together against our bodies. We hugged hard and then I looked into his eyes and we shared a kiss.

"Wow, oh fucking wow," he said.

The day after Mark and I had been running around naked on the sand bar I was at the swimming pool again, hoping he would invite me to get naked with him again. I was hoping Tommy and I would get together again soon too. I'd had a good day the day before.

"So what's up today?" Mark said as I stopped next to the tall lifeguard chair where he was sitting.

"Not much," I said looking down at the front of my swimsuit. "At least not yet," I said as I looked up and smirked.

"You little horn-dog," Mark said grinning.

"You liked it too Mark," I said.

"Yeah, you're right about that kiddo."

"You know my friend Tommy?"

Mark nodded.

"Yeah, the kid with the dark brown hair and eyes."

"We've been friends forever. Last night we sucked each other's cocks for the first time."

"No shit? You lucky little shit. He's cute as hell."

I grinned.

"I did pretty good yesterday Mark."

"Damn right you did. Maybe he'll want to play one of these days."

"He went to his granny's for a few days but when he gets back I think he'd be up for some naked swimming," I said.

Mark grinned and wiggled his eyebrows.

I looked at Mark's pretty feet right there in my face and remembered how I'd used them on either side of my cock to jack off with. I felt my dick begin to stir in my swimsuit.

"I better take a swim, I'm boning up," I said quietly.

Mark laughed and shook his head.

I dove into the water and swam around for a few minutes. I was just climbing out on the ladder below Mark's feet when I heard him say, "Holy shit, look at that." I got out onto the concrete and looked where Mark was gazing and saw a boy that I'd never seen before, walking out of the changing house. My mouth dropped open when I saw him and I gasped out loud.

"Mark, who the hell is that?"

"I have no idea," he said.

This kid was about the prettiest boy I'd ever seen. He had dark skin, like light chocolate and shiny black hair that covered his ears and hung down on the back of his neck several inches below his shoulders. If he hadn't been wearing a boy's swimsuit I'd have thought he was a girl, he was that pretty. He was very slim, but well proportioned and I watched as he hung his towel over the fence. He had silky looking armpit hair but not another hair on his body. The thing that really caught Mark's and my eye was his swimsuit. All of my buddies and the other boys in the pool were wearing cotton baggy swim trunks with a mesh thing inside that kept your dick from flopping all over the place. This kid was wearing one of those little tiny swimsuits that the speed swimmers wore, except instead of black like most of them had, his was bright orange. It was so small that it barely hid his ass crack and in front you could plainly see his dick, which was lying over to the left side and looked damn big. He might as well have been naked for all that the suit hid.

He turned and walked to the edge of the pool and dove into the water. I looked up at Mark.

"Holy shit, he's beautiful," I said quietly.

"No shit, I wonder who he is?"

"I'm gonna find out," I said.

I dove into the water and swam around making sure I kept the kid in my sights. When I got fairly close I dove to the bottom of the pool, swam along the bottom for a way and then swam to the surface, right under the kid. I ran into him as I surfaced, slamming my head into his belly.

"Oh shit, I'm sorry," I said. "I didn't see you I was swimming under water."

"That is okay," he said. "No harm has been done."

Hmm, he talked funny.

"Are you new here?" I said as I tread water next to him.

"I am visiting a relative who lives near here. I am from India."

"Wow, you're a long way from home," I said.

"Yes, I am but this was a good opportunity to see your beautiful country so I came here."

"What's your name?"

"My name is Raj,"

"Pleased to meet you Raj, I'm Danny."

"Pleased to make your acquaintance, Mr. Danny."

I laughed. "Just Danny."

I noticed Mark watching us.

"Let's swim over there and you can meet Mark, he's my friend."

Raj and I swam over to Mark and climbed out of the pool.

"Mark, this is Raj and he's from India." Mark looked down and extended his hand.

"Nice to meet you Raj."

"Thank you Mr. Mark, you are a very handsome man." Mark grinned. "I am fortunate to meet a person of authority who is so looking nice."

"Thank you Raj, but please just call me Mark. You are a very handsome boy too, how old are you?"

"I am 19," he said.

Wow, I'd have guessed he was about 15. While he and Mark were talking I was looking over Raj. He had the most beautiful skin I'd ever seen. It was light brown like a real good tan and it was so smooth and silky looking that I could hardly take my eyes off him. His face was very handsome and his eyes were deep brown with long black lashes. He had the whitest teeth I'd ever seen. As I was looking him over I looked down and saw his feet. Wow, they were beautiful. They looked like they were size 8 or 9, very slim and pretty with perfect toes and short nails. They were also very dark brown but the bottoms looked light tan.

I could barely keep my eyes off his swimsuit. He had a perfect bubble but and his suit had slid down a little revealing an inch of his butt crack. The wet material clung to his cock and it looked even bigger as I watched him and Mark chat. I took another look and realized it was growing. He was getting a boner as he talked to Mark. I looked up and saw that Mark had maneuvered his cock to the leg of his suit and had his legs apart, so Raj could see up the leg of his shorts.

I grinned up at Mark and he winked. "Raj, is staying for two weeks," Mark said.

"Cool, you want to hang-out?" I asked.

"What is hang-out?"

"You know spend time together, do stuff."

"Yes that would be nice. Will you hang-out with us too Mark?" As he asked he looked up Mark's pants leg again. Mark clenched his stomach muscles and made his dick jump a little.

"You bet I'm gonna hang-out with you two hotties," he said.

Raj looked at me with a questioning look. "What is a hottie?"

I burst out laughing. "You are Raj. Mark means a good looking boy like you."

Raj grinned. "You are very hottie too Danny."

Then he looked up at Mark, "I hope we can all have a good time together Mark."

Mark and I grinned.

"How about we go to the river tomorrow and spend the day on the sandbar?" Mark asked. "I'm off tomorrow."

I explained to Raj what the sandbar was and he was happy to go with us.

"I'll even bring some lunch so we can spend the whole day," Mark said.

Raj and I swam for a while and then he said he needed to meet his relative so he had to go. It was getting late so I walked with him to the changing house and waited while he got his basket with his clothes and I got my basket. I walked into the changing house with him. He put the basket on the bench and then pulled his little swimsuit down to his ankles and kicked it off. I stood there and looked at the prettiest butt I'd ever seen. His butt cheeks were just as smooth and round as they could be. I imagined my lips kissing those butt cheeks. When he bent over to pick up his suit I saw his little hole and it was smooth and hairless. I saw his nuts hanging down as bent over and wished I'd been able to see his cock. I was surprised when he turned around and stood there naked in front of me.

"Are you going to go back swimming or are you going to take a shower too?" he asked.

I was staring at his cock with my mouth hanging open. It was much longer than mine probably hanging at least 5 inches when it was soft. His cock was not circumcised like mine and his foreskin hung over the head. He had a perfect little black pubic bush and his nuts hung down quite far and looked to be as big as walnuts.

"I'm um, I'm gonna shower," I stammered.

"Do you enjoy the sight of my penis?"

"Yeah, it's very nice," I stammered.

Raj stood there looking at me. "Will you be taking off your shorts?"

I nodded. I hooked my thumbs in my shorts and pulled them down. Raj didn't hide the fact that he was checking me out. My cock was semi-hard but still hanging.

"You have a very pretty penis," Rag said.

"Oh thanks, you do too," I said.

"I see yours is missing the foreskin. That is unusual in my country."

"Yeah, they do that here when we're born," I said as my cock began to grow.

"I see you are becoming excited." Raj said. "Is it because you desire me?"

Shit, I didn't know what to say. "I'm um, yeah, I guess you're pretty cute and I do like you Raj."

He smiled. "I desire you also shall we go to the shower?"

It was late in the day and there were very few kids left in the pool so it was pretty safe messing around in the shower. We would hear the door open if anyone came into the changing room, so we walked into the shower room and turned on the water. We chose two spigots next to each other and stood there letting the warm water cascade down our bodies. The water running down Raj's body looked so inviting so I put my hands on his chest and began to rub his tits. Raj closed his eyes and I looked down to see his cock beginning to harden. I pulled him to me. Our bodies met and our arms went around each other. His body was so soft and smooth and I felt his cock moving against mine, which was now hard and sticking straight out. Raj put his hand on my cock and began to slowly jerk me off.

"You do that the same way we do," I whispered in his ear.

He grinned. "I think boys all over the world do it this way."

I put my hands on Raj's cock and it was also hard. It was as big as Mark's, which was about 7-inches. Raj's cock pointed up toward his belly and I looked down to see his foreskin had slid back revealing a light pinkish head on his beautiful boy cock.

"Raj you have a beautiful cock," I whispered in his ear.

"Thank you I like yours very much also."

We stood there jacking each other off and soon I felt my dick begin to tickle.

"Faster Raj, I'm going to cum." Raj moved his hand faster and soon my cock throbbed and a jet of cum shot out onto Raj's stomach. Four more shots of cum squirted out and then a little more oozed form the tip. Raj milked it all out and then licked off his fingers.

He smiled at me. "Your seed tastes very nice."

I began to jack Raj faster and he closed his eyes and leaned back against the shower wall.

"I am becoming very aroused. I will be ejaculating very soon," he said.

I leaned over and suddenly his cock jumped and I slipped my mouth over the head as Raj shot his cum. He squirted six or seven times into my waiting mouth and I sucked the last drops out of him. He was panting and opened his eyes to see my mouth on his cock.

His lips parted and he smiled. "That was amazing Danny."

"You're not grossed out that I sucked you?"

"Not grossed? No I am not grossed. I wish I had done so to you too though."

I grinned and opened my mouth. There was still cum on my tongue. "Want some?" I asked. Raj grinned and leaned forward and our lips met. His tongue snaked out and soon we were sucking each other's tongues.

"Uh hum."

Raj and I jumped and pulled apart. There was Mark standing looking at us.

"You horn-dogs are pretty brave," he said grinning.

"Sorry Mark we should have waited for you but we kind of got carried away," I said.

Raj looked at Mark's crotch. "Mr. Mark you seem to have a boner."

Mark grinned and stepped into the shower room. He pulled down the front of his swimsuit and his big boner popped out.

"Who wants this?" he said. I looked at Raj and he smiled.

"I would like very much to suck it," he said.

"Go for it," I said grinning.

Raj knelt in front of Mark and I walked to the doorway to keep a lookout. I could hear him slurping and then heard Mark gasp. A few minutes later Mark came around the corner with a flushed look on his face.

"Holy shit, that kid can sure suck dick," he said quietly to me.

I grinned. "So you're not mad at me for messing around without you?"

Mark leaned over and kissed me on the lips. "I could never be mad at you kid. I'm going to have a hard time sleeping tonight thinking about spending the day running naked on the sandbar tomorrow."

Mark wasn't the only one who would have a hard time all night but at age 18, I could jack off two or three times and still be ready for our naked day on the sandbar. It was proving to be a really good summer for swimming naked.

The next day Raj and I met Mark at the pool and we drove down to the river. We all three swam across the river to the sandbar and got naked in the willows. Raj didn't take any time getting naked, like he did it many times before. He seemed very at ease walking around with his dick standing up hard and ready.

"Many of my friends and I swim naked in a river near our city," he said.

"Do you have sex with them?"

"Yes with many of them. Boys often have sexual relations with each other in my country."

"That's how you got so dark?"

"I am naturally dark but I am darker because of the time I spend in the sun naked."

"You look like a native," I said.

"Do you find my dark skin attractive?" he asked.

"Yes, I do, it's very beautiful," I said.

"I find your light skin and beautiful blue eyes very attractive. Here in America there are so many different beautiful men. Some are dark, some are light, but all are very pretty."

He put his hand on my boner and began to stroke it. Mark stood there watching us slowly jacking his cock.

"Mark, join us," I said quietly.

Mark stepped up and soon we all were fondling each other. Mark and Raj began kissing and I dropped to my knees and sucked on Raj's cock. He began to moan when I did that.

I took Mark's cock in my hand and jacked him as I sucked Raj.

"I would like very much to have someone to fuck me in my butt," Raj said.

"Have you been fucked before?" I asked.

"Yes, I have friends in India that like to do this thing too," he said.

I looked at Mark. "Go ahead," I said.

Raj knelt on the sand and Mark knelt behind him. He pulled Raj's butt cheeks apart and smiled when he saw his beautiful butt hole.

"Oh man," he said. Then he leaned forward and began licking Raj's hole.

My dick was leaking like mad and Raj looked over his shoulder at me and motioned for me to kneel in front of him. He took my cock into his mouth and sucked me while Mark licked his asshole. Mark reached into his pack and pulled out a condom and rolled it on. Then he spit on his hand and he lubed up Raj's ass.

Raj moaned when Mark began putting his cock into his ass. He stopped sucking me but kept my cock in his mouth. Soon Mark was all the way in and Raj began sucking me greedily.

"I have wanted a penis in both ends of my body for a long time," he said. "This is a dream come true."

I put my hands on Raj's head and fucked his mouth. Soon I felt cum rising in my cock and pushed into him. I began shooting and he greedily swallowed as I came. Mark grunted and pushed into Raj's ass and held his cock there and I knew he was coming too.

We all collapsed on the sand in a big sweaty pile.

"Wow, that was like a dream," Raj said.

We lay there catching our breath.

"I'm all full of sand," Mark said.

"Let's rinse off in the river," I said getting to my feet.

We all waded into the river and rinsed the sand off our bodies. Raj was smiling at me and I felt underwater and found his hard cock.

"You need to cum," I said.

"That would be very pleasurable," he said.

We waded out of the water and I noticed Mark was hard again.

"Let's do another three-way," I said. "Raj can fuck me and I'll suck Mark."

They both grinned and we assumed our places.

I'd not been fucked before but I had put a carrot and a big magic marker in my ass when I jacked off and I knew I'd like it.

Raj had fucked before. He didn't even hesitate to lick my asshole. Mark got him a condom and soon I felt his big cock head pushing against my hole. The head slipped in and I gasped. Then Raj waited until I told him to go ahead and he slid into me and began fucking me. I took Mark's dripping cock into my mouth and slurped on it.

Fuck me. What a feeling. I'd loved the carrot but this was way better.

Raj didn't take long and soon he was slamming into me and I felt his big cock throbbing and emptying his cum into me. He lay on my back panting as I finished off Mark. Mark shot a huge amount of cum into my throat seeing as how he'd just cum a few minutes earlier.

Then we all lay together and rested again.

We washed off in the river again and lay in the sand for a while. I couldn't believe my luck being here with these two beauties. Raj's cock was so pretty when it was soft. It looked like a big tan tube resting on his hairless balls with his little pubes above it. I reached over and played with it.

"Danny, do you enjoy my penis?" he asked.

"Yeah, I do, it's really pretty," I said. Then I leaned forward and put it into my mouth when it was still soft. It didn't take long and Raj's cock began to grow in my mouth.

He leaned over and took Mark's cock into his mouth and soon Mark moved around and took mine into his mouth. We were doing a three-way suck. Fucking A!

"Since we're all hard again, how about I get fucked?" Mark said.

Raj and I looked up and grinned. "That is only fair," he said.

We ended up with Raj fucking Mark and him sucking me off. After another rinse we decided it was time for lunch. Mark had brought a blanket and we spread it out and had sandwiches and pops. It was so natural with all of us sitting naked in the sun enjoying ourselves.

"It's too bad more people don't get a chance to do this," I said.

"They don't know what they're missing," Mark said.

I kept looking at Raj's feet and they were so pretty.

"Do you desire my feet Danny?"

I grinned.

"I've got a little thing for feet," I said.

"My friend Yogesh also has such a desire. He likes to suck on my feet and toes when he masturbates."

"Can I?

Raj grinned and put his feet in my lap. I lifted them up and began kissing them and sucking his toes. Mark leaned over and took my cock in his hand and slowly jacked me off while I licked Raj's feet. It took a few minutes and I felt my cum ready to shoot.

"I'm about to bust," I said.

Mark leaned down and put my cock in his mouth and I unloaded cum into it. I put Raj's feet up against my face as I came. Damn what a sensation.

That pretty finished me off for a while so we took a naked nap. Raj was on my right and Mark was on my left. I looked at them, so different and both so beautiful. Life was good.

The next day was Sunday and I had to go to my granny's for dinner. Tommy was still gone but he was going to be back later in the day. Raj had to be with his family for the day so it was a dry day for cumming. Mark said he had to work but the pool only was open for a few hours on Sunday so he was gone by the time I got back from my grandma's.

Fuck, I hadn't cum all day and had half a boner all the way home. I decided to ride my bike down to the river and take a naked swim and jack off. I parked on the riverbank and checked to see if anyone was around. There was a boat with a couple of guys fishing downstream a long way but no one else. I stripped off my clothes and hid them behind a stump and swam across to the sandbar. It was late afternoon and a perfect day to lay around naked. I walked through the willows and came to the spot where Mark and Raj and I had fucked. There was a used condom in the bushes. I started getting hard.

"Well, I might as well jack off," I said to myself.

I sat on the edge of the sandbar on the side away from the riverbank and began slowly jacking myself. It felt good to work my cock and I wasn't in any hurry.

"Why didn't you wait for me?"

I jumped and nearly fell into the river. I turned and there was Tommy. He was naked standing right behind me.

"Jeez, you almost gave me a heart attack," I said.

He laughed.

"Man you were really going at it on your dick."

"Well everyone was gone or busy so I had to take matters into my own hand… so to speak."

"Well, let me help," he said sitting down by me.

I leaned back and Tommy took over on my cock. He jacked me and I could see him boning up.

"Wanta try sucking again?" I asked.

He nodded.

"Damn right."

"Lay down and I'll lay the other way and we can suck each other at the same time."

"Cool," he said getting up and turning so we were head to cock.

We took each other's cocks in our mouths and began sucking. Tommy's cock was great for sucking. While I liked Mark and Raj's big cocks they were hard to suck. Tommy's was perfect.

"Did you mess with Mark again?" Tommy asked.

"Yeah," I said.

"More sucking?"

"Yeah and more than that."

He stopped sucking me and looked at me.

"What more?"

"We fucked," I said.

"No way!"

I nodded.

"He fucked you in the ass?"

"Raj did."

"Who's Raj?"

I explained who Raj was.

"So this random Indian guy fucked your ass and you all fucked each other."

I nodded again.

"Damn. Did it hurt?"

"At first it did. But then it felt amazing. It's something that is hard to describe Tommy."

"Well fuck me," Tommy said.

"Okay," I said.

He grinned.

"You want to?"

"If you do."

"I want to."

"Do you want me to fuck you or you fuck me?" I asked.

"I want you to fuck me first."

"Shit we don't have a condom."

"Oh no, what can we do?"

"Wait," I said.

I ran back in the bushes and found the used one that Mark had used on Raj. I took it over to the river and poured out the cum and then filled it a couple of times with river water and rinsed it out. Then I rolled it back down and it was as good as new.

"Damn a used rubber," Tommy said."

"It was the one Mark used. It's okay," I said.

I could tell Tommy was pretty excited.

"So how do you want to do it?" I asked.

"There's a choice?"

"We can do it like a dog, or you can lay on your back and raise up your legs or I can lay down and you can sit on my cock."

"Holy shit. I like the dog idea," he said grinning evilly.

"Get on your knees bitch," I said laughing.

Tommy knelt on the sand and put his elbows on the ground. I pulled his butt cheeks apart. Holy smokes his asshole looked nice. It was pink and smooth and there were a few fine hairs around the edge of it. I took my finger and rubbed it.

"Oh fuck, that feels wicked," he said.

I put a gob of spit on my fingers and rubbed it more. Then I slid the end of my middle finger into his ass.

"Oh man," he gasped.

"Are you sure you want me to do this?" I asked.

"If your dick feels as good as your finger does, I damn sure want it."

"Have you ever put anything in there?" I asked.

"You won't laugh will you?"

I promised I wouldn't.

"I put a cooked bratwurst up there once."

I burst out laughing.

"You fucker you said you wouldn't laugh."

"Sorry, I didn't expect that. So you were just sitting around and decided to put a brat in your butt?"

"I had put my finger in there a few times when I jacked off and it felt really good. So I thought, finger good, brat better."

"Well that makes sense," I said chuckling.

"Are you going to fuck me or not?"

"Okay get ready," I said.

I put a gob of spit on my dick and put it against Tommy's hole. It looked like there was no way it would fit in there. I pushed a little and the tip went in. Tommy groaned.

"Should I stop?"

"Just go slow. Damn that feels huge."

"It is huge."

He laughed.

I pushed some more and the head slid into his hole.

"Oh God, hold it there," he said.

"Is it better than the brat?"

"Damn right," he said giggling.

I waited. I felt his ass ring clenching at my cock. Finally he said to put more in. I pushed a little and it went in another inch. I stopped and waited and then pushed in a little more. In a short time I had my pubes rubbing his ass and my balls were swinging against his.

"Oh fuck that feels full," he grunted.

"Should I take it out?"

"Oh fuck no. It feels great too."

I began pushing in and out and Tommy groaned every time I pushed back in. We got a good rhythm going and it didn't take long and I knew I was going to cum.

"I'm close Tommy," I said.

"What? You just let it shoot in there?"

"Yeah unless you want me to pull it out and shoot it on your butt or someplace."

"Shoot it on my face," he said.

"What? Really?"

"Yeah, right on my face."

I grinned to myself.

I felt the feeling and pulled out. I ripped the condom off and by the time I had it off Tommy had turned and had his face in front of me. I took hold of my cock and jacked it twice and it started squirting cum all over his face and into his mouth. I really shot a lot of cum.

When it stopped squirting Tommy grabbed my cock and stuck it in his mouth and sucked the last cum from the slit. He licked it off and grinned up at me.

"Yeah, now we're talking," he said.

He had cum all over his face and in his hair. I leaned down and licked some from his nose. He wiped some off with his finger and ate it.

"Damn that's good," he said.

Tommy jumped into the river and I jumped in right behind him. We washed the cum off us and crawled out on the sand and lay down next to each other.

"Damn Danny, that was hot," he said.

"You liked it?"

"I can't believe we've waited all these years to do this."

"No shit just think of all the cum we could have made."

"It would be gallons," he said.

We lay there a while and Tommy reached over and began fingering my ass crack.

"You want to fuck me?" I asked.

"You damn right I do."

I picked up the condom and rinsed it again in the river. We sure as hell were getting our money's worth out of this one.

I rolled it down Tommy's now hard cock.

"I want to do it on my back," I said.

He grinned.

"Okay, lay down."

I lay on the cool sand and lifted my legs up. Tommy knelt between them and ran his finger up my ass crack. He pushed a finger in.

"Damn that feels wicked," I said.

Tommy guided his cock to my asshole and pushed against it. I closed my eyes and felt him push and the head went in. He stopped and looked at me and I nodded. He worked his big cock into me until his balls were slapping my ass cheeks.

"Oh fuck that feels amazing," I said.

"Damn it's tight," he said.

I wrapped my legs around him and we fucked slowly and lovingly. Tommy was working up a sweat. He grinned down at me and I don't know for sure what happened but he leaned down and we began kissing. I wrapped my arms around him and hugged him tightly and we kissed while he fucked my ass.

"Oh man, I'm close," he whispered.

"Pull out and shoot it on my cock," I said.

He grinned.

"Kinky," he said.

Suddenly he pulled his cock out of me and pulled the condom off. He barely got his hand around it and it began squirting cum. He aimed it at my cock and balls and I began jacking myself. His hot cum lubed my cock and I began shooting cum in less than a minute. When I started cumming Tommy leaned down and sucked the end of it and caught a lot of my cum.

He collapsed on top of me. We lay there panting for a minute and then I kissed him on the cheek.

He turned his head and we kissed tenderly.

Tommy laid his head against my chest.

"Danny this is the most beautiful thing I've ever done."

I hugged him and kissed his neck.

"Me too Tommy, me too."

I felt so close to my friend. We'd been buddies for years but now it was different, something was happening to our friendship… it was becoming love.

I rode my bike to the pool the next day about 1 o'clock. It was just opening and I got in line to get a basket so I could change into my swimming suit. Tommy was up ahead of me in line and he looked back and smiled at me. I caught up with him in the changing house. He was sitting on one of the benches and seemed to be waiting for me.

"Hey," I said sitting down next to him.

"Hey," he said.

"So, what's up?"

He shrugged.

"I've been thinking," he said.

"About what?"

"Not here. I'll tell you later."

I nodded. We both took off our clothes and put them in our basket. I looked at Tommy naked and he was more beautiful than I'd ever thought before. His skin looked so smooth and lovely. His muscles seemed more pronounced. His ass looked magnificent. And, of course, his cock looked delicious.

He saw me perving him.

"You scooping me out?"

"Uh huh."

"Like what you see?"

I nodded. Then I licked my lips.

He took a good look at my cock and grinned.

We put on our swimming suits and turned in our baskets. Mark was sitting on the high chair at the diving boards. He motioned for us to walk over by him.

"Hey Mark, this is my best friend Tommy," I said.

Mark smiled at Tommy.

"I've seen you here many times but never knew your name. Nice to meet you Tommy."

"Likewise. Danny tells me you and he have become friends."

Mark grinned.

"You could say that. We've found that we enjoy," he looked to see if anyone was close, "swimming naked together."

Tommy grinned.

"So I've heard."

"And who would this lovely boy be?"

I looked and there stood Raj in his tiny little swimming suit. He was smiling his thousand-watt smile and getting an eyeful of Tommy.

"Raj, this is my friend Tommy. Tommy this is Raj, he's from India."

"The random guy who fucked you?" Tommy asked.

"One and the same," I said laughing.

They shook hands and looked each other over pretty closely. I noticed they both looked at the other's crotch pretty long.

"Tommy are you and Danny engaged in sexual gratification?"

Tommy looked surprised.

"Um, well we're friends and…" He looked at me.

"Raj, Tommy and I are very good friends. We have recently gone farther than just friends."

Raj mulled that over in his mind.

"So you are sexually active with each other?"

Mark laughed.

"Raj, you sure don't beat around the bush do you?"

"Excuse me, I do not understand. What is the bush?"

Oh boy.

Tommy, Raj and I swam for a while and then lay on the pool surround on our towels and sunned for a while. I lay there and looked at Raj, so beautiful and Tommy who I now saw in a different light. They were both gorgeous boys and I'd had sex with them both. How lucky could you get?

After a while Raj sat up.

"I must leave now," he said.

"Where are you going?"

"My relatives are making a cook out. They will be cooking the ribs of some animal on a portable cooking device on wheels."

Tommy and I grinned.

"Will we see you tomorrow?"

"Most assuredly. We will leave to go back to India in two days so I hope to make much sex before we leave. I am hoping we can do more naked swimming on the small forest in the middle of the river."

"We'll plan on it," I said.

Raj left and Tommy and I walked over to Mark.

"Raj is leaving day after tomorrow," I said.

"I'll get the day off and we can spend it on the river," Mark said.

"Cool, I think he wants to have a bunch of sex before he goes," I said.

Mark grinned.

"Speaking of that. What are you guys doing this evening?"

I looked at Tommy. He shrugged.

"What do you have in mind?"

"I've got the evening shift off. I thought a little naked swimming?"

Tommy and I grinned.

"We'll meet you about 6 o'clock right here."

"I'll bring the condoms," Mark said quietly.

Tommy and I changed into our clothes and got on our bikes and rode to my house. He seemed quiet. We sat in the lawn chairs out by the tent.

"What's wrong?"

"I've been thinking. You know we've been friends for so long. I've never thought of you as anything more than one of my best friends. But now I think of you and it's not just about being a fishing buddy. When I think of you I get a boner. I lie in bed and think of your cock and what we did on the sandbar and I get so hard. I'm not sure but I think I'm…"

"What Tommy?"

"I think of you all the time Danny. I think I love you."

My heart nearly burst. My friend was becoming my lover. I reached over and took his hand in mine and we got up and crawled into the tent. I zipped the door shut.

We knelt there facing each other and Tommy put his arms around me and pulled me to him. We looked into each other's eyes and then we kissed.

The first kiss was tender and then his tongue came into my mouth and I sucked on it. Then we swapped tongues and began kissing passionately. Our hands were all over each other and clothes began coming off. It didn't take long and we were both naked. Tommy lay back on the sleeping bag.

"Will you make love to me Danny?"

I nodded.

He looked so lovely lying there. He had his arms up over his head and his tufts of armpit hair looked beautiful. I knelt by his feet and took them one by one and kissed his toes and his soles. Then I kissed up each leg to his crotch. I kissed his belly and licked his belly button. Then I sucked on each of his nipples until they both stood up hard. Then I kissed his neck and sucked on his ear lobes. I kissed each eyelid and then kissed him on the lips.

"Fuck me Danny," he whispered.

I moved down and he raised his legs up. His hole was right there and it looked so pretty. I leaned down and put my tongue on it. Tommy gasped and looked down at me.

"Did you just lick my butt hole?"

I nodded.

"Damn… do it again," he said grinning.

I began licking his ass crack. I stuck my tongue into his hole and he moaned and groaned. I took his cock in my hand and it was leaking pre-cum like a faucet. I licked the pre-cum off and then put my cock at his asshole.

"I don't have a condom," I said.

"Have you ever done this without one?"

"No, have you?"

"I've only done it twice, once with you and once with Jessica and I used a condom both times."

"Then we're good."

I put some spit on my cock and put it up to his hole. It was already wet and my cock head went in pretty easy. Tommy gasped and wrapped his legs around me.

I worked my cock into him and soon my balls were slapping against his ass cheeks. Tommy had his eyes closed and was moaning quietly. I took hold of his cock and jacked him slowly.

"Tell me when you're close," I said.

We made love for several minutes. Tommy began to pant.

"I'm about to cum Danny," he said.

I was close too so I sped up a little and felt the tickle. I slammed into him and let my cock squirt into his ass. Tommy's cock began shooting cum and some went clear up on his cheek. We came for many seconds and then I lay on top of him. We were both breathing hard and sweating. I could feel his heart beating in his chest.

"Oh Tommy, that was amazing," I whispered into his ear.

"God, that was intense. I don't think I've ever cum so hard," he said.

We turned toward each other and shared a kiss.

Something was happening to us… and it was a good thing.

The next day we went to the pool and Mark grinned at us as we walked from the changing house. We walked up to his chair.

"What the hell have you two been doing?" he said quietly.

"What do you mean?" I asked.

"You're in love," he said.

"What? How can you tell that?"

"It's obvious to me. I see the way you look at each other. I see little smiles and touches. You two are falling for each other."

Tommy looked at me and smiled.

"He's right you know," he said.

"I know I'm right. And I think it's wonderful. A lot of guys your age have those feelings and suppress them and live their whole lives frustrated. I did that for a long time. I was twenty one before I finally gave in and admitted that I liked guys."

"Do you have someone now?" Tommy asked.

"I have a boyfriend. He's from Australia and had to go home for the summer to help his mom. His dad died this spring and he's helping with getting things settled."

"Is he okay with you… you know messing with other guys?"

"We decided when he left that we'd have fun during the summer. We're not the jealous type. When he gets back

I'll be happy to be with him. Until then... I'm always looking for cock."

We grinned and he moved his leg to let us see his cock, which was semi-hard and hanging in his left pants leg.

"It is most fortunate that I have found all of my friends here," a voice said from behind us. It was Raj.

"Hey Raj, how's it hanging?" I said.

He looked strange.

"It is hanging down and to the left a little."

We laughed. He took everything so literally.

"Maybe we can make it stand up," Tommy said.

"I was hoping that such a thing might be possible. Unfortunately my family has announced we will be leaving tomorrow and stopping in New York City to visit another relative, so I will only have today to enjoy your penis'."

"Oh damn," Mark said. "I can't get off today. We're one person short already."

"That is most unfortunate Mark. I would much enjoy to have your large penis in my bottom one more time."

"Well you'll have to settle for these two and their little dicks," Mark said.

"That will be sufficient," Raj said.

"Thanks for letting us have a say in it," I said laughing.

"I am much sorry. Danny would you and Tommy care to fuck my bottom?"

We laughed and nearly fell in the pool

Raj bid Mark farewell and we left with him to go to the river. It wasn't a long walk and when we got there we stripped off our clothes and held them over our heads as we swam across to the sandbar. We walked back into the willows. By the time we got there we all had boners.

"So do you want me or Tommy to fuck you Raj?"

"Yes."

"Tommy or me?"

"Yes, I desire both of you to fuck me."

"Who first?"

"Both of you."

"I understand you want us both to do it, but who do you want first?"

"I would like that you both fuck me at the same time."

"Huh?"

"I have done this thing at home in India. It is much pleasurable for me."

"Both at once? How the hell do we do that?"

Raj smiled. "I will show you."

He reached into his pants pocket and pulled out two condoms. He made a big deal of opening them and rolling one on each of our hard cocks. Then he got out a little tube of lube and lubed us both up and he lubed his asshole.

"Now if you and Tommy will sit here, facing each other and get real close together so your penis' are together, I will sit on them and you will fuck me together."

Tommy and I looked amazed to think he could take both of our cocks at once but we sat down and scooted together until our cocks were touching and our balls were mashed together between us. I put my hand around our cocks and held them together. Raj straddled us and lowered himself down until our cocks were in his crack. He reached around and moved our cocks back and forth until mine slid into his ass and then Tommy's followed. Raj lowered himself lower and in a minute he was sitting with both of our cocks buried in his ass.

Tommy and I sat there amazed. I could feel his hot cock against the bottom of mine and it felt very sexy. Then Raj began to raise and lower himself on them.

"Oh this is much nice," he said.

"I can't believe you can do that," Tommy said.

"I have done this many times. My friends at home do this all the time."

Raj was facing me and he leaned forward and I kissed him. Tommy reached around and took Raj's cock in his hand and began jacking him. Raj was sweating and moaning and it didn't take long for him to squirt all over my chest and belly.

"I'm about to cum," Tommy said.

I felt his cock throbbing and then I felt hot cum filling his condom. That set me off and I came really hard. Raj collapsed onto me and lay there on top of me. We all lay quietly for a minute and caught our breath. Then Raj stood up and there was Tommy's and my cocks with condoms half full of cum. Raj pulled them off us and poured the cum on our cocks and balls. Then he rubbed it in.

"Damn that's horny," I said.

We ended up in a big cum soaked pile kissing and sucking tits and limp cocks. After a while we were covered with cum and sand and we waded into the river and washed up.

"I will remember that when I am alone in India and pulling on my penis," Raj said.

"We were glad to have that experience with you Raj. You're one of the most beautiful boys we've ever seen and it has been a pleasure to know you and to have sex with you," I said.

"The pleasure has been all mine," he said.

We got our stuff and waded back to the riverbank. We dressed and walked back to town. Tommy and I walked Raj to his relative's house. We stopped a few houses short.

"Good bye Danny and Tommy. I will think fondly of you as I remember my time here."

We all had a hug and watched Raj walk down the street and go in the house.

"Wow, that was something," Tommy said.

"I didn't think that could be done. But now I guess we know it can be."

"It was fun but I'd rather be with you Danny," Tommy said.

"What do you think? Let's sleep in my tent tonight," I said.

Tommy had a wide grin on his face.

Tommy and I cooked some hotdogs on our campfire. We were in my back yard and sitting on a bench by the fire. We ate our hotdogs and then sat watching the fire and not saying much.

I knew Tommy had something on his mind.

"So why so quiet?" I asked.

"I'm just thinking of what we've done the past couple of weeks," he said.

"Regrets?"

"Oh no, I have no regrets except maybe that I wish we'd figured this out years ago."

I reached over and took his hand in mine. He smiled and kissed me lightly.

"Tommy I've always had a thing for you but I didn't want to take the chance of losing you as a friend," I said.

"I wish you had."

"I do now too. But now that we know how we feel what are we going to do about it?"

"I want us to be together. Does that sound silly?"

"Not a bit. I want us to be together too. But it's a big step. What about our parents and friends?"

"I don't know how to approach that Danny. I know that I want us to live together and be together all the time."

I looked into his beautiful brown eyes and saw the light from the fire dancing in them.

"We'll work it out," I said.

He nodded.

"Let's go in the tent and make love."

We got up and crawled into the tent. I zipped the door closed and we left the light off. We knelt in front of each other and wrapped our arms around each other and began making out. Our crotches were pushing into each other and I could feel Tommy's hard cock against mine. I took the bottom of his tee shirt and pulled it up over his head. He did the same to me. Then he pulled my shorts and underwear down and I stepped out of them. I took off his shorts and underwear and we embraced, our hard cocks rubbing together. I could feel wetness on his cock.

"Suck me," he whispered.

I sucked my best friend and then we made love long into the night.

"Who the hell is that?" I said to Tommy as we walked out of the changing room at the pool.

"Holy fuck, he's beautiful," Tommy said.

There was a guy standing next to Mark's lifeguard chair talking to him. He was absolutely gorgeous. He looked to be a little shorter than Tommy and me and had a body like a Greek god. He was very darkly tanned and his hair was long and golden blond. His face was flawless, with ice blue eyes and the whitest teeth I'd ever seen. He was wearing a pair of swimming trunks that had surfboards on them.

Mark said something to him and he looked our way and smiled. Tommy and I hurried over to them.

"Hey guys, this is my boyfriend, Kieran," Mark said.

"G'day mates," the guy said.

"Good, yeah, hi," I said.

"Um hello," Tommy said.

They laughed.

"I told you they were hot, I didn't say they were particularly bright," Mark said.

"Um, sorry you just surprised us," I said. "Mark didn't tell us his boyfriend was the most handsome man on earth."

Kieran looked at Mark and laughed.

"I like these guys already… before we've had sex."

Tommy and I looked at each other and almost shit in our trunks.

"What did you say?" Tommy asked.

"Mark told me he and you guys have been fucking this summer and suggested that he and I and you two do some naked swimming before the season is over. Mark only has a few days left before we head back to college."

"And we're gonna have sex with you?" I asked.

"If you want to. Mark says you guys are hot and sexy and I can see that plainly."

I looked at Tommy and could see his boner in his trunks. Mine was already sticking out.

"You better wrap a towel around those boners," Mark said grinning. "When I get off this afternoon we were hoping you two were free so we could go to the river and mess around."

"You fucking bet," Tommy said.

Oh man, it was going to be a long day.

Kieran, Tommy and I spent the afternoon swimming and lying on our towels in the sun. Kieran told us all about Australia and how he and Mark had met at school. I loved listening to his accent and watching him talk. He was one hell of a good-looking guy.

"So Mark tells me you three and some Indian kid had some pretty hot times this summer," he said.

"Yeah, the kid's name was Raj and he was a sex maniac," I said.

"That's what Mark said. He says you two are pretty hot too," he said winking at us.

"Did you do any stuff in Australia?" Tommy asked.

"I had a few blow jobs and a little fucking with some of my blokes who I used to mess with," he said. "Mark and I decided not to worry about a little extra fucking since we'd be apart all summer. We're not the jealous type."

"Tommy and I are just becoming… um boyfriends," I said.

Tommy looked at me and smiled sweetly.

"I can see you two look like you're in love. It's a good thing. Many blokes never find someone or are too worried about what someone will say about them with another bloke. Fuck them if they worry about it. They weren't your mates in the first place."

Finally the afternoon session at the pool was over and Mark could leave. He had the evening shift off. We all went to the changing room and stripped our suits off. Tommy and I were awaiting a look at Kieran's cock and it didn't disappoint. He dropped his suit and there was a beautiful uncut cock hanging under a tightly trimmed blond bush and over low hanging big balls.

"Damn," I said.

Kieran grinned and took his cock in his hand and pulled on it.

"Want some of this?"

I stepped forward and reached out.

"Not here you horn dog, wait till we get to the river," Mark said laughing.

I had a hard time stuffing my boner into my shorts.

We rode to the river in Mark's car. Tommy and I were in the back seat and we both were boned up. Tommy reached over and played with my cock through my pants. I had to make him stop because I was afraid I'd cum in my shorts.

When we got to the river we walked downstream along the bank and stripped naked and then swam across to the sandbar.

Kieran was ahead of us and I noticed he had no tan line. His ass was as brown as the rest of him.

"Did you do a lot of naked swimming in Australia?" I asked.

"Naked surfing," he said, his white teeth shining.

"Damn," Tommy said looking at Kieran's ass.

We got to the willows and gathered and began playing with each other's cocks. Kieran's boned up and it was about the same size as Mark's. As it got hard it stood up by his belly and the foreskin slipped back revealing a pink head. Tommy and I were mesmerized by it.

"Go ahead," Kieran said.

I looked at Tommy and nodded for him to go first. He dropped to his knees and took hold of Kieran's cock and licked the head. Then he pulled it down so he could get it in his mouth and began sucking it.

Mark took my cock in his hand then knelt down and began sucking me. I stood there watching with as hard a cock as I'd ever had. Kieran grinned at me.

"Nice fat cock," he said motioning to mine. "It'll feel nice in my ass."

Holy shit. My cock began to tingle and I began shooting into Mark's mouth. I must have surprised him because he kind of yelped. He went deep on it and let me squirt into his throat.

"Ah mate, I'm about to bust a nut," Kieran said to Tommy.

Tommy slurped on his beautiful cock and suddenly he jumped and I knew Kieran was cumming in his mouth. He didn't spill a drop. Finally Tommy let Kieran's cock slip from his mouth, partly soft.

"Whew," Kieran said. "Nice work mate."

Tommy grinned.

We switched places and Kieran took Tommy's cock in his mouth while I worked on Mark's big cock. I'd gotten used to it and could take almost all of it into my throat, which Mark really liked. Tommy had his eyes closed as Kieran worked on his dick and sucked his balls. It didn't take long and he began moaning and I could see Kieran swallowing. I went deep on Mark's cock and massaged it with my throat and he began shooting into my mouth. I milked him dry and then we all were ready for a little rest.

"How about a swim?" Mark said.

We all waded into the river and swam around laughing and splashing each other. Tommy and I grinned at each other. Shit just a short while ago I was secretly wishing I could see his cock and now we were lovers and spending time with two gorgeous college guys naked.

We got out on the sand and lay down in the sun. It must have been quite a sight. I'm glad no one came past in a boat or they'd have had a heart attack.

"This is our last time swimming naked," Mark said after quite a while.

"What? Why?" I asked.

"Now that Kieran's back he and I are moving back to our place at college. School starts in a few weeks and we're going to do a little traveling and a lot of fucking," he said.

"Wow, I didn't realize that but you're right, summer is almost over," I said.

"What will you and Tommy do?" Kieran asked.

I looked at Tommy and we neither had a clue. We hadn't talked about it.

"I don't know. I'm going to go to the two year school in Middleberg," I said.

"You are? I am too," Tommy said.

We grinned at each other.

"We've been so busy fucking our brains out we didn't talk about anything else," I said laughing.

"So maybe you two can room together?" Mark said.

"Yeah, maybe," I said. Tommy was grinning too.

"Well for a last time for us to be together for the summer, Kieran and I would like you two to fuck us," Mark said.

"Really?" Tommy said grabbing his cock.

"Really. We'd like to lay side-by-side and have you two do us at the same time."

My cock was half hard already. Tommy was fully boned.

Mark got two condoms out of his backpack and he and Kieran rolled them down our cocks.

"Who does who?" I asked.

"Rock, paper, scissors," Mark said.

"Winner fucks Kieran, loser gets me."

"That's not being a loser," Tommy said.

Tommy and I did it. I had a rock, and Tommy had a scissors. I won.

Mark and Kieran lay side-by-side and Tommy and I got below them on the sand. They raised their legs up and we looked down at their beautiful butt holes. Tommy looked at me and we both leaned down and licked their holes. The two of them had each other's cocks in their hands and were slowly jacking each other. Tommy and I moved up and we both put our cocks up to their assholes and in a few minutes we were fucking two beautiful guys on the sand.

Tommy looked over at me and we leaned together and kissed while we fucked. Kieran and Mark did the same. It was incredible to see these three beautiful guys all with me and all naked and having sex. I'd have never dreamed in a million years I'd be doing something like this.

After quite a while I began to get the feeling.

"I'm getting close," I said.

"Me too," Tommy added.

Mark and Kieran increased their speed on jacking and in the next two minutes we all four came. Mark and Kieran shot cum all over their stomach and Tommy and I filled our condoms half full. We lay forward and all ended up kissing each other in a big sweaty, cummy pile.

We finally got up and washed off in the river. We walked slowly across the sandbar to the river and swam across. We dressed and drove back to the pool so Tommy and I could get our bikes. Before we got out Mark said, "Well it's been a fun summer."

"It's been the best," I said.

"I hope you two stay together. You make a cute couple."

"We won't forget this," I said.

"We won't either," Kieran said.

"Maybe next spring break we can get together," Mark said.

"Wow that'd be great," Tommy and I said.

We traded phone numbers and had a quick kiss with both of our college boy friends. They drove off and Tommy and I stood there.

"Wow," Tommy said. "Fucking wow!"

"Now you're stuck with just me," I said.

Tommy looked to see if anyone was around. He put his arms around me and kissed me.

"Those guys are fantastic, beautiful, and sexy but I've got the guy I want," he said.

My eyes filled with tears and we kissed some more.

Tommy and I went to Middleberg to look at the college and see what they had for housing. We'd both been accepted in the school so now we needed to find someplace to live. We found a place that had been a motel and had been converted to student housing. The rooms were fitted with a kitchenette and were pretty Spartan but we thought it would work for us just fine. The only drawback was that the room was for a married couple or two people who didn't mind sharing a bed, because there was only one bed, a queen sized one. We were all for that.

Best of all the housing also had a pool and recreation building with games and a TV room. The price was pretty reasonable so we got the information and promised to let them know within two days if we'd take the room or not.

"What about our parents?" Tommy asked.

"What do you mean?"

"My mom thinks I should drive back and forth every day. She said it's only 20 miles and it's cheaper than a place to live."

"If we share the cost it's a lot less," I said.

"I hope you can convince her," he said.

We talked to our parents and they were skeptical to say the least. We were the first of our siblings to leave the nest and I think they felt like they wanted us to live at home as long as we could. Tommy and I wanted just the opposite.

That night Tommy asked his parents if I could sleep over. His room has a couch that is okay to sleep on so they said it was fine. After dinner we went to his room and played video games for a while. When the house quieted down we got naked and got into his bed and began making out. We were writhing around kissing and playing with each other's cocks and suddenly his door opened and his dad walked in.

He stood there for a second and turned and left.

"Oh fuck," Tommy said.

"I better go."

"No stay, you can't leave me like this."

We got dressed and sat with his TV on but not really watching.

There was a knock on the door.

"Yeah?"

"Tommy, Danny, can you come downstairs?" his dad said.

"Yeah right away."

He looked at me and I thought he was going to cry.

"What the hell are we going to do?"

"There's only one thing we can do. Tell them the truth," I said.

We went downstairs and were surprised when there sat my parents as well as Tommy's parents.

"Mom? Dad?"

"Sit down boys."

We sat side-by-side on the couch.

"I'm sorry I barged in on you boys a while ago," his dad said. "Obviously I didn't expect to see what I saw."

"Dad we can explain," Tommy started.

"Tommy, no explanation will change what I saw. We've talked and we may be old but we're not stupid," his dad said nodding to his mom and my parents.

"Danny, we've suspected you might be… not interested in girls for a long time," my dad said.

"We're not happy about the idea but we're willing to accept it," my mom said.

"We knew you two were good friends but didn't know about this," Tommy's mom said.

"Mom this just happened. Danny and I have never done anything like this until just recently. I thought I wanted a girlfriend and had some but it was never what I thought it was suppose to be. When Danny and I… when we found out we liked each other like this, it all became clear to me. I was trying to be something that I'm not."

"Tommy and I love each other," I said. "I know that's hard for you to hear but we do. We share all the things we've shared for our whole lives and now we share more than fishing and ball games. We're in love."

The parents all sat quietly absorbing it all.

"Well, how do we make this work?" Tommy's dad asked.

"We want to live together at school. We'd like your blessing on it and hopefully you'll get used to us being a couple," I said.

They looked at each other and seemed to be okay.

"So how soon do you have to sign the lease?" my dad asked.

Tommy and I were beaming. We had all we could do to keep from kissing but we held back. It might be too much for them.

Tommy and I have been living in our little room now for almost a month. We live on Hamburger Helper and Mac and Cheese mix, but have been watching the Food Network and Tommy is getting braver with trying some more exciting meals.

Today when I got home from class he was naked, wearing an apron to keep the hot grease off his dick, and making something he called "Tuna Supreme". He looked adorable with his bubble butt hanging out of the back of the apron. It didn't take long for me to get naked and in no time I was rubbing my cock up and down his butt crack with my arms around him.

"Stop that, you're going to ruin my dish," he scolded.

"Hurry up," I urged.

Tommy worked fast, looking at his recipe now and then and finally he announced the dish was ready for the oven. He opened the door and bent over to put it in. He yelped when my dick poked him in the ass while he was bent over. He shut the door and turned and slipped off the apron.

"We've got 45 minutes," he said.

We giggled like twelve-year old girls as we ran to the shower. We turned on the water and soaped each other up and then washed each other's hair. I knelt to wash Tommy's feet and his dick was right there in my face so I put it in my mouth and began sucking him. He held onto my head and fucked my mouth until he came into it. I got every drop and then stood up.

"Do me in the butt," I said.

He grinned and I turned around and held onto the showerhead and backed up. He got behind me and slid his dick in my ass and fucked me slowly under the cascading water. It was amazingly sexual.

Finally the water began to cool, so Tommy increased his pace and soon I felt him throbbing in my ass and knew he was filling me with cum. He pulled it out and we kissed and washed our cocks and butts and then got out. We dried each other off and walked naked to the room. It smelled fantastic.

"Chef Tommy, I think your tuna is ready," I said.

We sat naked eating "Tuna Supreme" and it was pretty damn good. Then we curled up on the bed still naked and pulled out our books and began studying.

I looked at him, his soft cock lying across his balls and his nose in a history book and my heart was full of love.

School is going fantastic. We're both working hard and getting really good grades. We figured if we do that our parents will be convinced that this is what is right for us.

Tommy and I have a great life. We love living together. We wake up and sometimes make love in the morning before class and a few times we've even come home for lunch and ended up naked and making love.

We got a call from Mark and Kieran and they've invited us to their school over spring break. We're really looking forward to seeing them again. They said to bring lots of condoms.

But the best part of our little home is that in the evening Tommy and I can sneak down to the pool late at night and take a naked swim. We've mastered making love in the pool and it's pretty damn hot.

Life is good. And with Tommy by my side, I can't ask for anything more. I'm glad I lost my swimming trunks that day in the pool when Mark found out about my naked swimming on the island. It led to an amazing summer of sex and to me finding the love of my life.

Made in the USA
Las Vegas, NV
14 June 2022